SEVERAL PERCEPTIONS

Angela Carter

virago

VIRAGO

First published by Virago Press in 1995
Reprinted 1997, 2005, 2010, 2011, 2012

First published in Great Britain by William Heinemann in 1968

Copyright © Angela Carter 1968

The moral right of the author has been asserted.

The lines from 'Dancing on the Ceiling' by Richard Rogers and Lorenz Hart
on p. 128 are reprinted by kind permission of Chappell & Co Ltd.

A CIP catalogue record for this book
is available from the British Library.

ISBN 978-1-86049-094-1

Printed and bound in Great Britain by
Clays Ltd, St Ives plc

Papers used by Virago are from well-managed forests
and other responsible sources.

MIX
Paper from
responsible sources
FSC® C104740

Virago Press
An imprint of
Little, Brown Book Group
100 Victoria Embankment
London EC4Y 0DY

An Hachette UK Company
www.hachette.co.uk

www.virago.co.uk

'The mind is a kind of theatre, where several perceptions successively make their appearance, pass, re-pass, glide away and mingle in an infinite variety of postures and situations.'

David Hume

Joseph was very poor at this time as he was giving all his money to beggars. One day, walking across the Down, he recognized an old man whom he knew who stood beneath a tree beside the Obelisk. This old man was small and slight. His snuff-encrusted, once brown, now buff, napless, styleless, ageless overcoat was straight and narrow as the path of righteousness. The tugged-down brim of his cap jutted like caves protecting the eroded sandcastle of his face from the furious elements that might otherwise wash it away completely. Grave-clothes small-clothes flapped around his legs like small, brown dogs, clearing his ankles by enough inches to reveal a purplish stretch of plucked fowl skin atop his old-fashioned boots, which were secured by several turns of string. All was gilded with visionary sunset light and the little old man appeared irradiated and just dropped from heaven. He was playing an imaginary fiddle as Joseph had seen him do before. Raptly he serenaded the tree, which dropped leaves on his head from time to time as if tossing contemptuous pennies. Beneath his feet, moist autumn grass blandly gleamed.

Joseph went up and stood beside him but the old man, only able to see invisible music, never noticed the young one. The veins on his hand stood out in whorled ropes as it flourished an imaginary bow. His other hand performed the fingering, his knotted fingers quivered like the wings of a humming bird, which flutter four thousand times a minute. He hummed a tune and beat out time with his left foot. It was hard to believe no fiddle existed. Old Sunny.

The pupils of Sunny's wet, round, hazel eyes were distinctly rimmed with grey and there was always a peevish redness about them, as if he were angry at being so old. He descended on the public houses like an ancient mariner questing a pliant wedding guest; his albatross was his great age and fascinating experiences as professional musician and man of the world, Sunny Bannister, a song, a smile, a melody, troubadour of mirth; Joseph had seen the old bills and programmes he always carried around with him folded up in his wallet. But he lied all the time; it was hard to tell where the lies ended and the truth began, or whether or not the press cuttings belonged to another person and old Sunny was not old Sunny at all but only pretending.

Three small children played near by with a rubber ball. They wore cheerful jerseys of blue and yellow wool and their sweet, shrill voices fizzed and sputtered like sherbet. Sunny once told Joseph how, when he was a child, all the nippers used to dance like Little Tich, stuffing the toes of their socks with paper to imitate Little Tich's long, pointy shoes. Now he was old and the children ignored him but he was still not much taller than a child of ten or eleven. Joseph stood close enough to him to catch a whiff of wintergreen; Sunny smelled of wintergreen by day but by night richly overlaid it with glucose stout. Joseph watched the old man's hands until he felt almost about to enter Sunny's dimension and would soon begin to hear the tune and see the fiddle grow in the air; Joseph was very tired and in a curiously disembodied state of mind, now and then glimpsing immense cracks in the structure of the real world. He rarely had a full night's sleep, since he was tormented with dreams.

This was one of his dreams. It was spring and he was walking in a formal garden. Tulips and children's heads were arranged like apples on a shelf in a store, in neat rows. The tulips swayed and the children smiled with red mouths. Innocent sunlight shone on everything. Along came a man in heavy boots and trampled down the flowerbed, both tulips and children; juicy stalks and fragile bones went snap. Blood and sap spurted on all sides. Joseph flung himself on the man and tried to choke him or gouge out his eyes but his hands made no impression for his body was, in the dream, insubstantial as smoke. When the last child's head was irrevocably smashed, the murderer turned his face to Joseph and Joseph realized he was looking at his own face. Then he woke up and broke his mirror so it would never tell the truth again, if it had ever told the truth before.

Joseph's eyes blurred with the poignancy of the light; everything starrily shone. He was on his way home from an extra spell of duty on the ward, his nostrils still full of mixed smells of excrement and Dettol, the textures of death still masking his hands. He leaned against the Obelisk, which was modest in size as Obelisks go, a memorial to a hero of the Nile shot beneath hotter suns. The Obelisk cast a touching small shadow across the grass, where shed leaves already rustled. The café on the corner twenty yards beyond the Down roasted its own coffee; this delicious, expensive, middle-class perfume curled seductively around Joseph like the memory of the girl Charlotte, with whom he associated it. It was not a scent he was accustomed to. In Brazil, home of much of the world's coffee, engines sometimes burned coffee beans for fuel rather than wood or coal when there was a coffee glut, another fascinating fact; Joseph ceaselessly grubbed out facts such as these if they might help to shore up the crumbling dome of the world.

The sun fell warm as gloves upon his slender, elegant hands which, an hour before, washed the last stains of mortality off a poor, dead old man and laid him out; although Joseph was working as a hospital orderly he retained a certain illegitimate intellectual status and could still construct a truth table, an elementary procedure in the study of logic. Nevertheless, he could not now remember whether Charlotte left him because he had failed all his examinations or if he had not bothered to attend any of the examinations anyway. He used to go into the library and feel like Goering to see so many books; he even set light to several, amongst them *Mansfield Park* and the Gospel according to St John, to both of which he had taken a particular hate. 'This is the time of the barbarians,' said Joseph, a typical barbarian, kneeling on the floor of the alcove where the dictionaries were kept and burning books with matches, applying the flame and watching with fierce joy as each page trembled and blackened; then he chalked upon a near-by wall the following slogan: SUPPORT YOUR NEIGHBOURHOOD ASSASSIN and went home to screw Charlotte.

Charlotte studied English literature; she composed endless essays concerning Jane Austen's moral universe whilst Joseph sat with a fey grin on his face contemplating new bizarre and ingenious methods of sexual intercourse, his only creative activity during this period of University life. Joseph had the chance of a fine education but threw it away; he had free choice on the self-service counter and voluntarily selected shit, old men dying, pus and, worse of all, most dreaded of encounters, the sweet, blue gangrene. None of which featured in Jane Austen's moral universe nor could be stylized as a truth table, alas. He toiled under a gangrene sky. 'The trivial round, the common task, would furnish all we ought to ask.' Every minute of the lonely nights was filled with dreams of fires quenched with blood and bloody beaks of birds of prey and bombs blossoming like roses with bloody petals over the Mekong Delta.

Joseph dreamed he was a child walking home from the Wolf Cubs down an ordinary street of privet hedges and clean milk bottles put out for the night under a fat, white moon but soon he realized a maniac with a knife was following him. The pace of the dream quickened; the child who was himself scurried and panted, quaking with terror, but the pursuer was relentless as the clock and gained on him; in and out of the shadows they went, in and out of moonlight. The blade of the knife flashed and Joseph saw the maniac's face was his own, himself. Mad for sanctuary, Joseph the child burst through a front gate and beat his fists on the nearest door. Which was immediately opened by himself again, smiling a long, narrow, wolfish smile as cruel as the knife he, also, carried.

Joseph was always surprised, in dreams as in the mirror before he broke it, to see his wary, sallow, ill-looking ferociously private face; was the mirror deceiving him or was he, in fact, dreaming about some other person and not himself at all, some comparative stranger from whom he had rented this secret face out of the Jacobean drama, Flaminco or De Flores, ambiguous villains. Yet his actual physical self, his flesh and bone, often seemed to him no more than an arbitrary piece of theorizing, a random collection of impulses hurtling through a void. Or else eyes without a face, eyes with behind them only a screaming tangle of raw nerves. Or (in certain ferocious moods of self-disgust) a big, fat, soft, stupid, paper Valentine heart squeezing out a soggy tear at the sorrows of the world.

He was often as sad, hopeless and full of baffled murderous thoughts as some animal in a very small cage. Once he went to the zoo and identified strongly with the badger. 'This animal bites'; who would have thought it, he was so furry. The badger was beautiful, wild and innocent but had apparently gone out of its mind for it ran ceaselessly round and round its tiny wire enclosure making small desperate whimpering noises from time to time. Joseph squatted in front of its cage for three hours watching it anxiously but in all this time the badger never took a rest. Round and round and round.

At last a keeper came up to Joseph and told him they were locking the zoo for the night. Joseph, unaware of the passing of time, explained: 'I'm watching the badger,' thinking perhaps the keeper might let him stay a while longer. 'Why is that?' asked the keeper. Round and round and round ran the badger, whining. 'To see if it disappears up its own asshole!' cried Joseph, stung to white-hot fury by the keeper's insensitivity. On the other hand, he felt no sympathy for the smug gorillas, at the best of times nothing but self-satisfied exhibitionists, nor the big cats who rotted fatly in their pens at ease as if in love with captivity. The black panther, for instance, had given away so much of its self-respect it now resembled nothing so much as an overstuffed sofa badly upholstered in rusty plush. But the badger continued to whicker: 'No surrender!' and after all these years still searched for a way out although Joseph could no longer go and see him as things with the keeper went from bad to worse. He could not remember how it happened but an ugly scuffle occurred and now Joseph was not allowed in the zoo at all.

However, 'while there's life, there's hope'; Joseph was still keeping up appearances, still clean and shaven, still tidily if shabbily dressed. He was twenty-two years old and lived with a white cat, a handsome and prolific she. Once a year, at Christmas, he hitch-hiked home to make the gestures of affection although he went in fear and trembling; he could not remember when his parents' house first began to menace him.

His father was a newsagent and tobacconist who worked hard

all his life. His mother was just an ordinary housewife who worked hard all her life. At home he sat in an uneasy chair urging the plaster ducks to try and fly across the wall. There was a tooled leather *TV Times* cover and a brass Dutch girl concealing fire-irons in the hollow of her back. These things seemed wholly threatening; the leather cover was a ravenous mouth smacking brown lips and the Dutch girl must use her little brushes and shovels as cruel weapons since there was no other use for them; the room was heated by electricity. His bewildered father surveyed a son who was hardly there at all and said from time to time: 'But we've always done the best for you, I can't understand it,' while his mother, with the odour of roasting turkey caught in the springes of her hair, remonstrated: 'Don't go on at the boy, Father, after all, it's Christmas.' Would the sizzling bird flutter out of the oven if it could, even if its heart were gone, replaced by forcemeat, nor any head left, either. Maybe it would, if he furtively opened the oven door and muttered: '*Sauve qui peut*.'

But Joseph knew it was too late to save himself from shipwreck, though, so far, from day to day he managed to survive, hanging on to daily images of pain and fear at the hospital for some kind of daily bread. His own acts of patience and gentleness with the old men in their extremity seemed the only real things he did; cleaning the dying and laying out the dead were acts of profound innocence and even love and all the diabolical horseplay, the filth and indignity surrounding death also seemed a black kind of innocence. And there were moments of sweet peace, as on the Down, leaning against the warm stone, watching the aged musician caught in the solid honey afternoon light like a fly in an amber of eternity. The granite surface of the Obelisk stood out in golden grains like rare bark of gold where it caught the sunlight and the children laughed and played. Oblivious to everything outside the rectilinear parallelogram of his overcoat, Sunny played sweet inaudible tunes in extra-dimensional opera houses and Albert Halls of the imagination.

> Such, such were the joys
> When we all, girls and boys,
> In our youth time were seen
> On the Echoing Green.

Joseph was so tired he closed his eyes for a moment and might have gone to sleep like Napoleon standing up but immediately there arose a terrible storm and clamour of shouting and abuse, Sunny's cracked old voice swearing horribly and calling down terrible vengeances upon the little children; the shell of calm which had contained them all was shockingly broken.

The children's ball must have hit Sunny. It was already too late to tell whether this had happened accidentally or on purpose but, however it occurred, it knocked off his rarely-doffed cap, and a huge dog, sprung up from nowhere, had seized the cap between its teeth. It ran round and round Sunny in circles, wagging its tail; it had the best of intentions and wanted to organize a game of some kind, perhaps. It was a tall, brindled, square, broad-shouldered dog built like a fur tank, about half the whole size of Sunny, with big cocked ears like the paper tricornes in which Joseph's father served two ounces of sweets. Sunny, rudely jolted from a dream of music, lunged after the dog with forlorn cries but the dog always escaped. The imaginary fiddle was dropped, broken or lost. The absent cap revealed a thick mop of iron-grey hair on Sunny's head; Joseph was surprised as he had guessed Sunny to be existentially bald beneath it. The three children abandoned their ball and leapt about in glee, shouting.

Joseph stepped forward to rescue the cap but the dog loved fun and, unwilling to stop, turned tail and fled at a great rate, still

n the cap, and Sunny stumbled after, swear-
n went off dancing round them. So away they
left alone, faced with a simple moral situation,
knew, to his shame, he would.

very well he was not going to follow the travelling
atch back old Sunny's cap and return it to him; he was
oing to perform this simple act of comfort for an old man
ause a miserable anger filled him with weary boredom. An
npathetic little wind, chilly with winter, ruffled the grass and
pulled down some handfuls of leaves. He shivered in his threadbare coat. He wanted to vanish, sleep, fade. Braving dreams,
down into the black rabbit hole or hole of Calcutta of sleep; yet,
in the cold wind, he knew he would not survive much longer,
the current took him nearer and nearer to rocks with teeth like
sharks. So he left the green edge of the Down and went home.

It was a once-handsome, now decayed district with a few
relics of former affluence (such as the coffee shop, a suave place)
but now mostly given over to old people who had come down
in the world, who lived in basements and ground floor backs,
and students and beatniks who nested in attics.

All the old people seemed to be out taking the air this afternoon. Everywhere Joseph looked, he saw old people with sticks
and bulging veins in their legs and skulls from which the flesh of
their faces hung in tattered webs; they advanced slowly as if this
might be their very last walk. A man with a metal hook instead
of a hand passed by and then a hunchbacked woman.

Many of the shops were boarded up, to let, or sold second-
hand clothes, or had become betting shops but, nevertheless, this
street had once been the shopping promenade of a famous spa
and still swooped in a sinuous neo-classic arc from the Down.
Plaster mouldings of urns and garlands decorated upper storeys of
rusticated stone and rosy brick where tufts of weeds and grass

sprouted from every cranny and broken wi[...]
patched with cardboard, if at all. The pavem[...]
green and white with droppings of fat pige[...]
among the maimed and old as smugly as if the[...]
seen the last of its good times long ago.

Up this vista came a striking couple, mysterious Beve[...]
and the plump Rosie, giggling in soft, geisha voices and ti[...]
the bells of the bicycles on which they rode. Beverley Kyte[...]
always called Kay by his friends; he possessed a deceptive appea[...]
ance of extreme youth and was scarcely any taller than Old
Sunny. He wore Levi jeans and jacket weathered to the beautiful blue of very old and often handled five pound notes. On his
head he wore a khaki forage cap and golden ear-rings glinted in
his ears. The rest of his outfit comprised: a flannel shirt, lacking
a collar, probably bought at or stolen from a jumble sale then
dyed a cheerful orange in the communal spaghetti saucepan;
green round wire-rimmed sunglasses; dirty white plimsolls; and
a blue enamel St Christopher medallion round his neck, together
with a doorkey on a piece of string and an iron cross. Somehow
he gave the appearance of being in costume, like a little
Superhero, maybe Mini Man or Mighty Moppet biking off to a
meeting of Teen Titans.

Joseph knew the name of his companion because she often
wore a teeshirt with the name ROSIE stencilled unevenly on it in
black; today she wore a teeshirt printed with the legend: CANA-
DIAN NECKING TEAM. She also wore jeans and a broad-brimmed
hat of battered black felt. She was small with apple cheeks, long
black curls and a dreamy expression. She and Kay swerved about
in the roadway, tinkling and giggling; motorists hooted and
shook their fists. Kay was starting a moustache, there was a vague
sepia shadow on his upper lip.

Kay had this peculiarity, he always looked entirely content.

This often seemed to Joseph a personal affront, especially when he saw him unexpectedly. He never spoke to Kay; even in the old days when Joseph was more extrovert and went to parties, the sight of Kay and his little retinue of friends and hangers-on laughing and smiling together was enough to plunge him in gloom and he would think with distress of the habits of kytes, fierce birds of prey. He had never attended any of the Dionysiac revels Kay held in the shabby mansion where he lived, a great Georgian palace friable with worm and rot.

This house was the mausoleum Kay's dying mother had created for herself, full of tatty splendours. A footlights favourite of the 1930s, the world she knew was shot down in flames in 1940, although her husband, Mr Kyte the fighter pilot, was not himself shot down until 1945. There was some money somewhere, some investments, a pension. A veteran of numerous forlorn hopes such as art school and the catering trade, Kay was now content to live at ease among theatrical relics, sell a little pot from time to time and keep open house for friends who came and went like ships that pass in the night.

Meanwhile, Mrs Kyte died a little further, a few more inches, each year, swimming so deeply in drugs she did not know one year from another; but Kay always looked as happy as Larry and dressed up in fancy rags and rode around on a silver-painted bicycle accompanied by his fat, compliant bird. The sweet tintinnabulation of bicycle bells shimmered into the golden haze of distance, it was like the sound of happiness. Joseph, in shreds of darkness, bowing his head beneath many of the troubles of the world, thought of wounds opening like rosy mouths.

And there was nothing to do but walk down this street of hard, menacing angularities and brutal forms. He passed fresh carcasses in butcher's windows and displays of knives. When he came to the fishmonger's shop, he remembered there was no food at home for his cat and dared to run the gauntlet of cruel claws of crabs to buy her half a pound of coley, the cheapest fish. She ate from a dish marked Pussy and lacked for nothing, sleeping upon his own pillow. As Joseph pushed the slithery packet in his pocket, he bumped into Sunny again as he went out of the fish shop. Sunny cannoned right into him.

He was on his way back from the Down. He was in a fury which made his dance a private mono-dance of offended dignity and hurt pride; he huffed, mumbled, coughed and spat. His curious eyes were bloodshot with rage. He was oblivious to everything except his humiliation. He was still capless, the dog or the children must have got it; without the cap, he looked only partial, an amputee. He shivered and shook, might shake apart in the furious autumn of his flesh.

'Watch where you're going, boy,' he said without smiling, rocking backwards and forwards on his feet; he caught hold of Joseph to stop himself falling. Joseph, almost overwhelmed with wintergreen, righted the old man and, wheezing and coughing, Sunny grew a little calmer.

'Give us a fag,' he ordered brusquely. 'Give us a fag, I'm clean out. I could just do with a fag. What an afternoon!' At the memory, he began to tremble again. 'Give us a fag!'

Joseph fumbled in his pocket and found a pack of ten, still full, cellophane even unopened, taken from the locker of a man who, being dead, had given up smoking. On the other hand, false teeth, spectacles and watches were scrupulously returned to the bereaved of the deceased; when Joseph asked what happened to glass eyes, they were peremptory with him, as though he had committed a breach of taste.

'Here,' he said, reaching out the pack. 'Have these, take the packet, old skip, old Sunny.'

Sunny immediately let go of Joseph's arm and straightened up to his full four feet ten inches; his mask of grimy wrinkles and his wet red eyes expressed affront too deep for anger or tears. The gift, it seemed, was the cruellest cut of all.

'Don't you patronize me,' he said, with impressive grandeur. 'I'm old enough to be your grandad.'

With a very proud gesture, he struck the cigarettes from Joseph's hand on to the ground and crushed them with the stamps of his holey boots.

'I only wanted the one fag,' he said. 'I'm not a bloomin' beggar. It was only one fag I wanted, don't force your charity on me. I was the equal to Kreisler in my time and played before crowned heads. I don't want your patronage.'

Proudly Sunny stumped away. His boots went thump, thump, thump, like heartbeats. His hair was a grey flag at half mast; his coat was coffin-shaped. Soon he was lost to sight among the shoppers. The pavements were still gilt with sunset but now the cold wind was shrewish and nagged. Joseph stared down at the smashed cigarettes and tawny spilled tobacco; he was in a condition to fear omens and to obey mysterious voices in his head or on the wind. He remembered every word of Sunny's reprimand with beautiful clarity.

And it was positive proof of something he had, in his worst moods, always suspected. That the old men despised his tenderness, maybe even hated him, because of his compassion; he had no right to play fellow traveller on their last journeys of degradation and misery, no one had any right. Joseph watched the wind finger the fragments of trampled tobacco and thought of the condemnation in the eyes of the old men, how in this world of pain all he could do was wipe away their filth and pity them. Pity them. And nobody had any right to pity them, in the world of no expiation.

He continued home. Joseph was living in a small cave at the

top of a rearing cliff of stucco, a huge, elegant terrace or crescent curving into the side of a hill; but here the iron embroidery of balconies bled rust in wet weather, surfaces of paint crackled and peeled and flaked and plaster-work crumbled away continually so this twilight region of one-room flats had a leprous and mice-nibbled look. Joseph lived in an attic or garret, sharing kitchen and bathroom on the floor below; thirty shillings a week unfurnished and, when it rained, tears from heaven leaked through his roof. When it was sunny, Joseph and Charlotte used to sit on the little parapet among the eaves like king and queen of a counterpane country, for all the city was laid out before them, a very expensive toy indeed.

At the foot of the hill of crescents and terraces flowed the river with a barge or boat upon it; here the city dock and all the cranes and warehouses reflecting themselves in stretches of dark water; there white lines of the flyover buzzing with traffic; the prim red inexpressive grids of housing estates; and surrounding everything a rim of sweet green hills, low and round as if Joseph and Charlotte had moulded them from plasticine. Now this panoramic toy appeared and disappeared in mists of autumn, a boat softly blew its horn, the traffic noise was insubstantial as the drowsy hum of bees as Joseph let himself into his room and home.

Charlotte and he painted the room and lived in a pure bubble of whitewash until they fell out; now the walls were grimy, yellowed and mysteriously figured with stains of rain. There was a narrow mattress on the floor; his tumbled sheets were grey with dirt and smelled of flesh. There were few possessions in the room and these were hardly of a personal nature. They were such things as a discarded tennis shoe, an empty light ale bottle and a pair of sunglasses with one lens cracked. A washstand (yellow wood and streaky bacon marble) held a few withered paperbacks, a textbook on logic, Gilchrist's *Life of Blake* and *Alice in Wonderland*, which Charlotte gave him, signing it with love. Also some new books about the war in Vietnam and an untidy pile of newspaper cuttings on the same subject, both of these scrawled over and over with notes and exclamations in red ink of Joseph's gangling handwriting. Also a book on British wild life which fell open at a chapter on badgers. And several scrapbooks in which he had cut out and pasted facts.

There were some pictures tacked to the wall. Lee Harvey Oswald, handcuffed between policemen, about to be shot, wild as a badger. A colour photograph, from *Paris Match*, of a square of elegant houses and, within these pleasant boundaries, a living sunset, a Buddhist monk whose saffron robes turned red as he burned alive. Also a calendar of the previous year advertising a brand of soft drinks by means of a picture of a laughing girl in a white, sleeveless, polo-neck sweater sucking this soft drink through a straw. And a huge dewy pin-up of Marilyn Monroe.

A picture of Charlotte was tacked over the gas fire. She was squinting into past suns. Her blonde hair blew over her face which did not in the least resemble the face he remembered, since that face reincarnated in fantasy after fantasy, recreated nightly in dreams for months after she left, had become transformed in his mind to a Gothic mask, huge eyeballs hooded with lids of stone, cheekbones sharp as steel, lips of treacherous vampire redness and a wet red mouth which was a mantrap of ivory fangs. Witch woman. Incubus. Haunter of battlefields after the carnage in the image of a crow. After the bombs fell, in the ruins of the village, the rescue party surprised a woman gnawing gobs of flesh. His Madonna of the abattoir. But this was not always so; during the months of love, they struggled to entirely lose themselves in each other and make of each other's bodies a kind of home, since home is where the heart is and there is no place like it. But then she went, vanished as completely as if she had always been a fantasy, and these malignant ghosts came gibbering around his bed with dreams of charnel house unions which caused his waking mind to scream.

The electric bulb lacked a shade, the harsh light cast no shadow. A built-in wardrobe by the fireplace sagged open under the pressure of the dirty laundry which crammed it full. There was a strip of brown old carpet worn through to warp and woof in front of the fire. There was an ink-stained table with a kitchen chair pushed under it and another chair with splintery arms and a broken leg on which stood a Mickey Mouse alarm clock with a loud, shrill, nagging tick; in his mind, he called this clock 'Charlotte'. Everything bloomed with dust. The room had the feel and smell of a waiting-room at a railway station where few if any trains stop. Joseph was entirely surrounded by the banal apparatus of despair.

He filled the cat's saucer with milk and went down to the communal kitchen to boil her fish. There was no sign of the cat herself. The kitchen contained two cookers and a sink. The cat went in and out of the house through the window, which opened on to a fire escape at the back of the house, so this window was always left open and the kitchen was always very cold. There was a shelf with brown earthenware teapots in a severe file. The floor was always littered with spent matches. Joseph had one saucepan of his own which he used for the cat's fish and perhaps to boil an egg for himself now and then. His eggs always picked up the savour of fish, this seemed to him a Japanese taste. He never cooked more elaborately than this. He put the fish in the saucepan, filled the pan with water and set it on the stove. All his actions, the click of metal against metal, the spurt of water, the rasp of a match, sounded unnaturally loud. The smell when the fish began to cook caught his throat. He leaned against the open window and looked out over the roofs, gardens and dancing lines of washing for a glimpse of his cat coming home.

She was fine, handsome and white as paper. She had two litters of kittens a year; she sat purring and serene as the furry commas blindly sucked her flanks, and tottered about and cried in sharp, small voices like tiny knives scratched on very small plates. Then they were weaned and Joseph gave them away to the pet shop, who sold them. He had not been able to define his moral standpoint on whether or not to keep the kittens and could not afford to feed them all, anyway. He looked for his cat but she was nowhere to be seen, probably slaughtering some defenceless pigeon or harmless mouse; she was not soft-hearted.

He saw there was a new teapot on the shelf, a little red enamel one, and a brown teacosy which had not been there before now hung from a hook. A new tenant, probably in the room beneath his own at the back of the house, which had been vacant for some time. He rarely saw the other tenants, everybody kept themselves to themselves, although he often spoke to an old lady on the ground floor who smiled at him because she envied his cat which she surreptitiously fed with tid-bits though she had little money to spare for treats. She had such thin, white hair, the rosy skull shone through. She told Joseph the pater was an admiral so she had the sea in her veins; she had seen better days but now she had nothing, not even a cat or a photograph album or a few locks of hair in an envelope for everything she possessed had been destroyed in the war.

Joseph noticed the new tenant had sewn a name tag into the teacosy so that nobody would steal it, a very feminine thing to do. A. Blossom. Probably a secretary, in her thirties or forties, lonely, winter descending on her face, scattering crumbs for birds on her windowsill and his cat would come and kill the birds as they perched pecking. Well, he did not want to meet

A. Blossom tonight and he might not be there tomorrow; and in this way, this cool and casual fashion, he decided the time had come to end it all. When the fish was cooked, he turned it out on to a plate, boned it carefully and carried the reeking dish upstairs. Still no sign of the cat. It was growing dark; his room was full of autumn and cold. He knelt in front of the gas fire. As soon as he touched the tap, he realised that what he would do next was as simple and obvious as the place where the last piece of sky in a jig-saw puzzle should go.

First, however, he took the cat's food and milk saucer outside the door so that she would get a meal that night, for he did not want the cat to suffer, she was an innocent carnivore. He wondered if he should leave a note for his friend Viv to look after her but decided Viv would take charge of the cat out of warmth of heart without the melodramatic compulsion of a hand from the grave. Joseph contemplated his grave; it looked to him as in a cameo, an urn by a willow, beside it, a girl in draperies, an utterly chastened and totally etherealized Charlotte, weeping copious tears. He dismissed this fancy.

When he turned the tap and caught the first whiff of gas, he had vague second thoughts; to die of ennui and despair, instead of for some cause, with some motive, making some humanly significant gesture, was a grey, sad way to go. It was a simple way of saying 'no', that nothing was worthwhile. Then he saw the flesh of the monk in the eternity of the photograph, how it continued to burn for ever. Viv would find his body, blue at the extremities, such was the effect of coal-gas poisoning; Viv was serene and would not understand, Viv was flesh, which was grass, as it said in the burial service (which would not be said over him). The gas hissed, the die was cast.

Death, be not proud; it was not proud, it came into his room invisibly, insidiously, at once, streaming from the unlit fire. No cortège with plumes and mutes, no ritual. Adieu, farewell, earth's dubious bliss. Coal gas in its present form is lethal because of the carbon monoxide it contains; under normal conditions, the blood absorbs oxygen to form oxyhaemoglobin but in the presence of carbon monoxide it will ignore the oxygen completely to form carboxy-haemoglobin, another fact he had learned somewhere. I am i' the way to study a long silence. These tags of literature had nothing to do with the matter in hand; he could not make the act of dying significant to himself through the charming rhetoric of men who had never performed it for themselves.

All was unreal, this room, this smell of gas, this thin, pale form squatting before the fireplace on the bit of carpet, huddled in its own arms because it was so cold. He had only seen the act of death perpetrated upon the very old, that is, real death, a fact and not imaginings, photographs, news-reels and hallucinations, real death in bed. This fact of death was for old men such as his grandfather, who was dead, and the old man he had laid out, who seemed now to wear his grandfather's face; he was cheating time, pulling a trick on mortality. Gas and darkness slowly gathered in the room. Joseph waited for oblivion, which was slow in coming. The busy alarm clock ticked away the last beats of his heart.

'You bitch,' he said to Charlotte's photograph. 'Little do you know I've got the upper hand at last!'

A dead lover is in the strongest position of all since the remorse of grief will make a stone throb like a heart. Above the fireplace scowled disgruntled Charlotte, snapped one Bank Holiday in the very park where Sunny lost his hat today, beside the very Obelisk, where the fuse of his dissolution had mysteriously been lit. The more he looked at the photograph, the angrier he became, and there would be no further chances to see it. He rose drunkenly to his feet and abused the photograph with vile language. Viv's mother was on the game in a high-class, exclusive fashion; her hobby was drinking, when drunk she moved slow and stiff, as Joseph moved going to tear up Charlotte's picture so she would not spy on his death, which ought to be a private thing.

He could not think nor reason nor explain afterwards. In this anti-world of imminent departures were strange flora and fauna of the antipodes of the mind, where concepts stood on their heads. It was a world of paralogic and irrationality. Gas and air in certain proportions, 1:12 gas/air, is highly explosive, a true fact.

'I'm on my way,' announced Joseph to the ripped up fragments of Charlotte, always a literary girl. 'However, I shall go, not with a whimper but with a bang, you bitch.'

He struck a match. 'Gas is funny stuff,' said the lugubrious fellow who mended the fire, 'you never know where you are with gas. Best not to mess around with gas, you know.' He laughed, he suggested Joseph did his homework more thoroughly next time; himself, no doubt, learnt roles such as the grave-digger in *Hamlet* and the porter in *Macbeth* in his spare hours. 'You'd never have gone this way, anyway,' he said. And anyway, the blasted windows showered a hard rain of glass on to the pavements below and through the jagged gaps came rushing the sweet evening air.

2

In spite of soothing drugs and barbiturate sleeps, visited by dreams of the bottom of the sea and peaceful dark, Joseph could not assimilate what had happened to him; when he was delivered home and lay in his own bed again with his round, white, lollipop, bandaged paws flat out on the crisply turned back sheet before him, he was still astonished that, although well washed and neatly laid out, he did not otherwise resemble a corpse. Somehow, he thought, he had contravened the laws of cause and effect, as the philosopher Hume suggested was possible; he had blindly stumbled upon a formula that annihilated causation and now anything was possible, rain would fall upwards and sparrows begin to recite the Apocalypse in throaty voices of bards and prophets. He lay still on his mattress while Viv puttied in a final sheet of new window glass, whistling as he worked.

Viv was natty and hirsute; like the vivacious and intelligent Saki monkey, he parted his hair beautifully in the centre and sported a luxurious moustache and imperial. It was eleven o'clock on a blowy, shiny, cool October morning. Joseph's room was entirely changed. For one thing, it was sparkling clean; for another, quite white again. Viv had painted it out besides scrubbing the floor and laundering the clothes for Viv's time was his own and he had no work to go to, subsisting upon unemployment benefit. There was a brisk, pleasant smell of soap and new linen. Joseph noticed the explosion had cracked the face of his alarm clock right in two and delivered it such a visceral shock it had stopped short, for ever recording the moment the gas ignited, five past five, which would always be the time in this room, now. On the mantelpiece six ferocious bronze chrysanthemums in a jam jar cast an intricate shadow arborium against the wall where Marilyn Monroe still smiled like the Queen of the May. 'Well, I've missed my chance of meeting her,' thought Joseph morosely, for here he was, sick, shocked and shaken, padded out in a grotesque clown costume of bandages but still alive.

His beautiful cat sat on his pillow and made her ablutions as if nothing had happened, moistening her crooked paw and washing behind her ears, which were a rosy gold powdered with white, the colour of Turkish delight, and faintly translucent. When her ears were perfectly clean, she washed her face, which was pointed; she looked like an albino lynx. Today her nose was a deep pink. The colour of her nose was by no means constant; some days it just faintly flushed with a tenuous shelly pink, hardly a colour at all; other days, this sensitive organ with which she learned so much of the world was brighter than a peony. When she was a kitten and so small she could stand on Joseph's palm, her nose had been a vibrant maroon. She was a slender, sinuous cat, with ballet-dancer paws. Down her front were eight nipples; tight pink buds concealed in softest hairs. When stroked or fondled, first she purred ecstatically and then grew bored and bit and scratched the caressing hand with mouse-destroying teeth and claws. She left a track of shed white hairs everywhere she sat; she was subtle and unpredictable as a hallucination. Joseph looked at her with the dazzled eyes of the newly reborn; any minute she would tell him secrets.

'You're a lucky son of a gun, my star,' said Viv conversationally. He spoke the drawling accent of the city and used all the local endearments, my queen, my lover and my star. He lived happily with his mother in a bleak, luxurious flat over a car salesroom by the river; he often remarked, 'I know my mum's the neighbourhood love machine but there's room in her heart for me.' He was well-adjusted and sweet tempered. He was a musician and played the piano and organ.

'This was your life,' continued Viv obliquely. He was the glass of fashion and the mould of form in a pin-stripped suit of navy blue, a Mafia-style shirt of rough black silk and a fatly knotted lilac satin tie. Joseph watched him without understanding him, as he was watching the cat, in the ambiguous sunlight.

'Now you see me, now you don't,' suggested Viv, trying in his elliptical way to tease out a reason for Joseph's act. The sunlight cast white shadows on his black hair, glossy as a well-polished boot. He received no answer and at last shrugged and sang out: 'Poor old Joe.'

'The light hurts my eyes,' said Joseph.

'You've got no blinds,' pointed out Viv. He had quite finished the window and stood back to admire it; there were palmprints and fingerprints all over the new glass which he proceeded to industriously polish away with a huge white silk handkerchief unfurled from his breast pocket.

'The bird downstairs brought you them flowers,' he said. 'She brought them up in the jam jar, what a kind thought, eh? Flowers for you to come home to. Lovely blooms, real prize blooms.'

'What bird?'

'The bird downstairs who found you, I told you.'

'Oh,' said Joseph. The girl in the flat on the floor below, the newcomer, possessor of the knitted woollen teacosy, had heard a muffled bang which set her light-bulb dancing on its flex, discovered Joseph charred and unconscious, sent for an ambulance and then effaced herself completely, he did not even know her name.

'The bird downstairs,' repeated Viv, neatly knotting the ends of this conversational loop and glancing around with a faintly self-satisfied air. The cat sat up on her haunches like a cross between a lynx and a kangaroo and busily licked her front, studded with its eight pink rosettes (which team did she support?).

'What's this girl called?'

'Annie, Anne, something like that, she looks like a little orphan Annie, poor kid. She's got a terrible limp. She's nothing to write home about, I can tell you, but she's got a kind heart, or so it would seem.'

The new glass was now so clean as to appear invisible. Viv put away his improvised duster and sat down cross-legged at the foot of Joseph's mattress; all his movements were succinct and elegant, he performed even the most commonplace acts with the air of a circus acrobat, as if confidently expecting applause, and now everyone in the room was contained on Joseph's mattress, they could all go to sea together, using it as a raft, if the tide came in the window.

'I shall call you Lazarus, my star,' said Viv gently, lighting a cigarette.

'I certainly came back with a bang.'

'Though nobody called you.'

'That snap of Charlotte went up.'

'Just as well. Let the dead bury their dead.'

'I had a go,' said Joseph, viciously. After that it became necessary to change the direction of the conversation.

'Mum got you some nice new sheets. She worries about you, you know. She said you'd catch typhus from the old ones.'

'Typhus?' repeated Joseph, perplexed.

The cat, vibrating with purring, completed her toilet and curled up for sleep but continued to purr for a long time after her eyes were closed. She curled up in the curve of Joseph's shoulder and presently began to warm him with her glowing body heat; a cat in a sack would make the best hot water bottle in the world.

'The cat looks glad to see me home,' hazarded Joseph, hoping against hope.

'Cats wear smiles painted on permanently,' said Viv. Then he coughed and asked politely: 'Did you fall or were you pushed?' Meaning, was it an accident or a decision; he was too tactful to come right out and ask why his friend should want to kill himself, after contriving to get by for so long.

'Do you remember Charlotte?' sidetracked Joseph.

'I remember Charlotte, yes, she was a very good-looking bird, in her way, all blonde bone and hauteur. But she wasn't very nice to that old man in the pub you used to talk to, that awful bore, old Sunny, she just used to sit and sulk when you chatted to him. And she'd never talk to me, just look at me disgusted because when she met my old lady, my old lady said "Pleased to meet you" and then went and was sick all over your Charlotte's shoes, which were green suede and hardly worn. Ruined with sick, her shoes were, she never forgave me for that. Of course, Charlotte wouldn't look at me in those days but things would be different now I'm in a group. It's amazing what middle-class girls will do for you when you're in a group, dropping their drawers isn't the half of it.'

He took a small comb from his breast pocket and passed the time in combing his hair although it was already as sleek as p.v.c.

Joseph watched the hairs on the back of Viv's hands and wondered if they picked up messages from the ether.

'All the same,' opined Viv, 'you've left it a bit late to pack it in because of Charlotte walking out on you, she went a good six months ago.'

'I only asked if you remembered her,' said Joseph gently.

They were silent; Viv smoked his cigarette, Joseph lay between stiff, new, cool sheets in a room never before so clean and full of flowers, a totally changed room, and whenever he thought of the explosion, was overcome with shame and embarrassment. Death was certainly not proud, nor even dignified; he was just a practical joker or fool with bells and bladder and Joseph no tragic suicide but a furious august now done up in comic swathes like the Michelin man, such indignity. He tried to explain his disastrous sense of anti-climax to the psychiatrist, who wore spectacles with flesh-coloured rims. 'I feel as if Pilate had ordered a last minute reprieve and I'd gone all through that for nothing.' The psychiatrist took off his glasses to polish them, he revealed colourless eyes like pressed flowers and his name was Ransome. 'May I call you Arthur?' asked Joseph. 'Why?' asked the doctor in puzzlement and Joseph knew in a flash they could never be friends. Ransome encouraged Joseph to ramble down Memory Lane. There Joseph met his grandfather.

His grandfather was a clerk on the railways and always wore a blue shirt and a separate starched collar as white as snow with a shine on it like mica. He could make handkerchief rabbits jump out from his armpit and used to bring alive a whole shadow menagerie on the floral wall of Joseph's bedroom by means of his eloquent hands during lonely sleepless nights of toothache or earache in very early childhood, when these performances seemed like real magic. And he would give Joseph a Fox's Glacier Mint to suck when they went to the common together to watch cricketers or footballers, depending on the time of the year, on a Sunday afternoon. These memories seemed to Joseph to have the peculiar beauty and truthfulness of very cold water.

'These sweets had a drawing of a polar bear standing on an ice-floe on the wrapper,' said Joseph. Ransome listened but said nothing. 'My grandad would always point this out to me and say, "Gladly my cross I'd bear; here is a picture of Gladly, my cross-eyed bear." When I was four or five, this reduced me to tears of helpless mirth but now just to tears.' The old man died of cancer of the rectum, possibly the most humiliating death of all. Joseph often saw his grandfather's face on top of blooms in the cancer garden of the hospital. When Ransome heard this, he made a note on his pad.

'How about some tea?' suggested Viv, combing his flowing moustache. 'A nice cuppa?'

'Do you remember your grandfather, Viv?' asked Joseph vaguely, remembering the smell of clean old man, soap and pipe tobacco.

'Are you trying to take the piss?' demanded Viv suspiciously, dropping his comb; he was illegitimate, his father nameless, and his mother's family would have nothing to do with her. Recollecting this, Joseph was sorry he had been thoughtless and hurt the feelings of his one surviving friend but there was nothing to say, nothing that could be said. Such collisions of non-communication as this had made Joseph, little by little, give up attempting relationships. Viv went huffily off to boil the kettle.

The room seemed very bare now that everything was put away neatly; besides, Joseph had hardly any possessions although, when Charlotte lived here, the room was full of things, posters on the walls, prints, pictures cut out of magazines, old-fashioned coffee grinders, a pot for making Turkish coffee. Which she did occasionally to spite him. They had numbers of twanging discords; she would use cookery as a weapon just as if she were working-class. Once, after he had done some particularly extraordinary sexual thing to her, he caught sight of her glaring at him mutinously and she said: 'You're only trying to humiliate me because my father is the director of several companies'; then she put garlic in all the food for three weeks. Once the room had contained innumerable Mexican paper flowers, Indian felt rugs and print bedspreads, enamel mugs, casseroles, ashtrays, all kinds of clothes, cushions, records, magazines, newspapers, any friendly amount of clutter; most of these things were Charlotte's but some belonged to him. The Frescobaldi albums. Robert Johnson, King of the Delta Blues. A stuffed owl in a glass case. A horse's skull they found on the Mendips, quite bare of flesh and brain, reduced to nothing but bone and space. They found it in the lea of a dry stone wall where, years ago, the horse must have died of exposure one winter.

Joseph used to gaze at this skull for hours. He would look at it until it ceased to resemble a skull at all and became an abstract bleached lunar landscape of crevasses, caves and promontories, and through these winding bone passages he could retreat past caves filled with sleeping bats through successive backward generations of the ancestors of man, back to the beginning of the world. Here colours were hardly dry on things and foxy ten-toed eo-hippos munched incredibly green leaves of forests of the Tertiary period, snuffing delicious odours on the new winds, and Cain had not yet slaughtered Abel so time had not begun. In his mind, Joseph always reckoned time as starting the moment of the first murder. So this horse's skull seemed to Joseph a very innocent and important thing but it had vanished like everything else, one could be sure of nothing. It must have fallen through some metaphysical hole in matter like all those comic books, where were they? At one time, he had possessed four hundred and thirty-seven comic books and read and reread them continually; his favourite character was the Incredible Hulk, a noble savage with unusual qualities of brute force and dumb loyalty. He sat and read comic books while she sat and read F. R. Leavis and from time to time the farcical nature of their mutual preoccupations (she was looking for truth, he was looking for perhaps innocence) – these preoccupations would oppress him, he would rise up and jump on her.

However, all gone. And 'The Well Tempered Clavier', his favourite piece of music; and somebody stole the record player, unless it belonged to Charlotte, anyway. Somewhere, somehow all these things had uncreated themselves or maybe gone back to nature, the leaves of books through pulp back to rag and even further, perhaps to white balls of cotton as voluptuous to the touch as his white cat's front or to tall trunks of blue fir trees; the skull of the horse, secreting brain cells, a mane, a tail, cantering off, whinnying; and woollen clothes gone back to fleece of friendly sheep.

'I used to have quite an extensive wardrobe,' he said to Viv, who returned and began to pour the tea. Joseph had three plastic cups, and two saucers. The cups were deeply stained on the inside from tannin. 'What happened to all those clothes I had?'

'You gave 'em away to tramps, my lover,' said Viv, smiling sadly through a puff of fragrant steam.

'And all those comic books, where did they go?'

'Out of fashion, my star.'

'Jesus, am I as superficial as all that?'

'No, my lover, but quicker off the mark than most.'

The tea smelled fresh and nostalgic as it had smelled at five past five long ago, when his grandfather cleverly cut piano keyboards for him from pieces of bread and butter and Dan Dare flickered on the television set.

'I wonder what they mean when they say one has to become a little child again to enter the Kingdom of Heaven.'

'What, are you thinking of having another go, then?'

So they were quits as far as spitefulness went. Joseph could cope with his cup if he sat upright and wedged it firmly between his bandage gloves. There were lots of pillows, some retaining a ghostly female perfume; Viv must have brought up some extra ones from his home, perhaps pillows against which his mother, Mrs Boulder had been screwed for money.

'How are you feeling now?'

That was a hard one to answer; he had formed a random pattern, just as he fell after the explosion, a chance formation which he could not read. Sunny Bannister once told him he had owned a laughing cat that went ha! ha! ha! This cat was run over by a car and all its brains spilled out but, quick as a flash, Sunny scooped them up in his hat and thrust them back into the skull and soon the cat was as good as new; but, instead of laughing, it barked. Bow! wow! wow! Joseph appreciated the painful disorientation of this unfortunate cat as he had never appreciated anything before.

'Like pieces in a kaleidoscope or colours in a prism, perhaps.'

But there was a difference, the catastrophe had reduced him to an absolute, self-derisive humility. Now even the idea of meaning was abandoned; nothing was sacred and, since there was no reason for his arbitrary resurrection, there was no significance in anything he would do again, all his gestures were hollow like those of a bad actor. Yet there was a certain serenity in this emptiness, some kind of arid nourishment in the empty spaces and dry air of this Arabia Deserta of the heart where all the clocks were stopped.

'That little bird was in the kitchen,' said Viv. 'I tried to chat her up a bit but she wasn't having any, she was washing out a few things.'

'Mm?'

'This chrysanthemum girl. You know. I said to her to come and visit you. "He won't bite," I said but she didn't say anything. If she does, be nice to her, don't snarl; remember, she saved your life.'

A curious sanctimonious expression crossed his face when he said this but the simplicity of the fact, that some strange girl saved his life without asking her permission, appalled Joseph.

'What do you think she saved me for? If she saves enough suicides, will it buy a guide dog for the blind?'

'I shouldn't think you've been returned for a special mission from the chief,' snapped Viv. 'Why are you so sorry for yourself? Listen. I read this in *Weekend Mail*. You can have it for your collection of fascinating facts but there's a moral in it for you.'

He stood in the middle of the floor and recited formally:

'Matthew Buchinger, known as the "little man of Nuremburg", was only twenty-nine inches high and had neither hands, legs, nor thighs but this dynamic little German is still, after well-nigh three hundred years, a lesson in man's ability to overcome infirmity.

'Born on June 2, 1674, the last of nine children, he soon learned to play the flute, trumpet and dulcimer and at length even contrived to master the bagpipes! Using the fin-like extremities which served as his arms, he became a fine penman and also drew landscapes, portrait sketches and coats of arms. He showed a winning streak at cards and dice, could play ninepins and shaved himself without aid.

'And — most marvellous of all—he became one of the greatest conjurers of his time. During his performances of magic,

31

Buchinger presented the cup and balls trick, requiring tremendous dexterity, and many other feats of sleight of hand. His charm of manner made onlookers forget his infirmities.

'And this mighty magician was no laggard in love. Married four times, he fathered eleven children.'

During this account, Joseph became increasingly bored and irritated; Viv finally ceased and fixed him with a faintly accusing, brown, liquid stare, the regard of a man in a secure, if unconventional, moral universe.

'That was an Uncle Tom of the deformed,' Joseph said truculently, threshing about in his bandage diving helmet. 'His life was one capitulation.'

'Some people can cope with their afflictions,' said Viv, conscious his task was wasted. 'It's not even as if there was anything wrong with you, you impotent bastard, you just complain all the time.'

'Barnum offered Sarah Bernhardt a million dollars for her leg. I bet she was glad to cut it off.'

'What's biting you?'

'Nobody knows,' said Joseph. 'I can't explain.' He vanished completely under the bedclothes, under the pillows of Mrs Boulder's shame. There was a long silence. Then Viv, obviously determined to change the conversation, began:

'You know them little nurses in their caps like halos, well, I had one. I had that little redhead. From County Cork, she was. She was just coming off duty so I took her out on the Down and it was quite nice, really, ever such a nice day, you'd never have thought we'd had our summer.'

Joseph began to moan silently.

'I never say no when it's offered.' Viv coughed modestly and added: 'She swore she'd never seen equipment the size of mine, not even professionally, in the wards, that is; she suggested I should leave it to the nation, for the Natural History Museum. We had quite a laugh.'

He poured fresh tea and fanned it delicately with his wide-brimmed Fedora. Once he started talking about sex, he always found it hard to stop.

'Of course, I'm poking that Rosie whenever I get the chance, you know. She doesn't say much but she smiles a lot, you get the impression you're communicating.' Suddenly he cried out as if struck with a sudden brainwave: 'Here, what you need is a bit of bird!'

At the stark notion of sexual intercourse presented out of the blue, a vagina on a salver, Joseph shrank up to the size of the kernel of a nut and began to repeat over and over again: 'Shut up, shut up, shut up,' but nothing could halt Viv in this mood.

'All over the world, at this very minute' (consulting his wrist-watch) 'people are copulating like buggery and here are you, celibate as a vegetable marrow since Whatshername buzzed off, no wonder you've got in such a mess. Here, I'll bring that Rose round some time, I'd have a bash at her if I were you.'

He was full of simple good will but Joseph was so horrified by the startling obscenity, sex in his filthy dressings, Hieronymus Bosch encounters beneath the burning eyes of the monk on the wall, he howled out loud and cast around, deliberately this time, to hurt his friend.

'I wouldn't say no to your mother,' he said.

'You couldn't afford her,' said Viv serenely. 'She's got a very high-class clientele.'

'Then why aren't you rich?'

'It's the booze, isn't it. Poor old mum.' He sipped his tea, crooking his little finger, but in spite of his assumed nonchalance it was apparent the shaft had struck home when he added in a more subdued voice than usual: 'As a matter of fact, Joseph, I don't think it would be too friendly of you to knock off my mother.'

Viv's mother had a bright white steeple of curls on top of her head; this fragile construction slid sideways as she drank during the course of an evening while the bright peach false face she assumed upon her natural features began to run with moisture until she looked like a pink stucco Venetian palazzo about to subside in a cascade of mud and rubble into a canal. Only the eyes remained invariable in the disintegrating façade; her eyes were startling and forlorn, grey as rain, the eyes of a miserable young girl trapped (not knowing how) in a strange, ageing, garish cage of flesh. Once, in the pub, when Viv was absent for a moment, she leant across the table so Joseph had the impression of tumbling down the shadowland no-mans-land between her gigantic breasts and kissed him full on the mouth with a great play of lips and tongue. Joseph remembered Hippolytus and resolutely refused to explore any avenues which might open up, for Viv's sake, but there was no sequel to this episode; she stayed in the splendid isolation of her haunted silences and kept her hands to herself.

'All the same, you're welcome to Rosie; she believes in saying "yes" to life.'

'I just go up to her and say "Let's affirm" and give her a poke, do I, just like that.'

'You'd probably have to talk about the weather for a minute or two first, of course.'

He poured yet more tea with gestures straight out of a chimp's tea party. Viv preferred to perch on the arms of chairs and to nibble all round the edges of a biscuit as he twisted it about in his furry, simian hands. His centre parting was no whiter than his teeth. He always made himself perfectly at home. Now and then, Viv's supernatural good humour seemed to Joseph to be in the worst possible taste; after all, he was Kay's friend, they laughed and smiled together.

'You're my ray of sunshine,' said Joseph sourly.

'Well, maybe I'll get you some hash off Kay, that'll do you a bit of good.'

'I saw Kay on a bicycle the other day looking like the happiest man alive.'

'After all, he went to a progressive school, he isn't like us,' Viv pointed out.

'I'm not supposed to go back to work at the hospital,' said Joseph. 'Ransome said all I saw there was screened in glorious Kafkascope, only he didn't say so in so many words, of course. What shall I do when I'm up and about again?'

'You become a parasite on the state, my lover, just like me; it's the twentieth-century way to live.' He sighed and put on his hat and gnawed his fingernail; he had to be gone, his group, the Electric Opera, was rehearsing.

'Is it all right to leave you, do you think.'

'As long as you take away the matches.'

All the same, Joseph was full of guilt because Viv was so anxious to care for him and Joseph could only brood and snap in return. And how he was alone for the first time for weeks, free of nurses and the distressing auras cast around by patients (from the Latin *patior*, to suffer, whence we also derive the word passion), and the sun shone. A clot of blood heat, the cat lay in the hollow of his shoulder. A wind rose up and blustered against the window with a horrid noise which, after a while, Joseph identified as that of gunfire in the distance. Therefore another audial hallucination; Ransome refused to allow him to admit the idea of visions. However, the gunfire grew louder; he heard it more and more clearly. Until the commencement of hostilities, Vietnam was called the rice-bowl of Asia but now they had to import their food since chemical flame seared the tender crops, to say nothing of the tender flesh, and the bullets rattled although Joseph knew all the time it was only the wind knocking to be let in. And whether he heard the gunfire with his real ears or not, nevertheless, over there the bullets flew and the bombs dropped, just as the old men continued to die although he was not in attendance in a white coat like Ransome's to lay them out. It was not a case of out of sight, out of mind. Then there came a little scratching at the door.

'Who goes there?' demanded the cat mutely, immediately starting up; her ears went together back to back like spoons to listen behind.

'Who's that?' asked Joseph, in the grip of nameless fears. No reply except a sexless cough. Joseph shivered in his sheets. The wind bumped against the panes. Marilyn asking him to come home, all was forgiven.

'Do you want to come in?'

The door swung open. He was expecting any kind of spirit or emanation but his visitor proved to be a perfectly ordinary young woman he had never seen before. She carried a yellow Pyrex dish with a spray of deeper yellow roses on the side of it. Her head drooped down. Her brown hair was a permed frizz. She wore a clumsy suit of grey flannel with a skirt an inch below her knees. She stood in the doorway and seemed reluctant to look at Joseph, which, considering how grotesquely he was decked out, seemed perfectly natural to him.

'I live below and there is a custard in this dish,' she said. Her voice was flat, low and unmelodious and her accent Midlands. 'I made this custard with eggs and milk. I made it specially.'

She presented the dish with a brusque, ugly gesture. The cat leapt from the mattress and ran to sniff her feet; she moved from foot to foot, trying to avoid the cat, disliking it.

'Well,' said Joseph, utterly bemused. 'A custard. Well.'

He effortfully shifted part of the way upright in bed, in order to look at her from another angle since he was seeing her as melodramatically foreshortened, like a portentous shot from a German expressionist film.

'Custard is good food for building you up.' She still had not raised her face. In her old-fashioned clothes, she could have been almost as old as Viv's mother but she was far less interesting to look at. There was a long pause. And this was the woman who had saved his life. In view of this terrible fact, there was little small talk to be exchanged between them; they had only one topic in common.

'Where can I put this custard down safe?' She would not look into his eyes; he was grateful the custard existed, as they could converse about it.

'Put it down on the table. Yes, that's right. That's very kind of you, that's a very nice thought.' His voice petered out.

As Viv had said, her left leg was stiff and she limped noticeably. He saw her face at last and it was bleak and pale, she was no beauty. It was an anonymous face in the crowd, face of a girl with a paper carrier bag of groceries waiting at a rainy bus stop or the blurred newspaper face of a girl raped and murdered by a perfect stranger while walking by herself in a wood; it was a plain brick in the wall of the world. She set down the dish. There was no sound but the wind again. She was plainly anxious to be gone but too shy or too ungracious to know how to make her exit.

'I suppose,' said Joseph at last, grudgingly, since it had to be said, 'that I must thank you for calling the ambulance.'

'It was no trouble,' she said frostily.

'That certainly puts things into perspective,' thought Joseph.

Under her square shouldered jacket, she wore a round-necked jumper of dingy pink wool and a string of artificial pearls. He surveyed her with mixed feelings, indignation uppermost; she was the Orpheus who dragged him by hook or by crook from the underworld, in a sense his second mother since he had re-entered the world again through her.

'I'll tell you a fascinating fact,' he said. 'The same year the city of Saguntum was destroyed by Hannibal, a child was born who took one look at the world and returned immediately into its mother's womb.'

She jumped perceptibly to hear the word 'womb'.

'You'll find it in the elder Pliny.'

'Bring back the dish when you've finished with it,' she said abruptly. 'When you're on your feet.'

They looked at each other as blankly as creatures of different species.

'Is there anything I can do for you?' she asked ungenerously.

'Well, I suppose you could pass me a book to read. From the case. Anything will do to pass the hours....'

At random, she chose *Alice in Wonderland*, which was apt since she looked a little like Tenniel's Alice, severe and proper, but cropped and singularly lacking in charm. Her hand was shaking as she placed it by the bed, perhaps because she was disturbed to be alone with a strange man or perhaps for some other reason; she scuttled to the door.

'I don't know your name,' said Joseph, struck by the oddness of the fact.

'Blossom. Anne Blossom.' She spoke without any warmth in her voice as if the words only accidentally referred to herself. She quivered and went out without saying anything else. Although her name was Blossom, she was by no means a flower, unless so tight in bud she would wither before she bloomed. Her thick, high heels went clumping down the stairs. And Joseph recalled he had not thanked her for the chrysanthemums which blazed away on the mantelpiece. It was hard to imagine Miss Blossom stepping into a flower-shop and selecting such shaggy, leonine, dynamic monsters; one would have thought pinched bunches of violets or sepia bouquets of dry everlasting flowers would have been more up her street. The chrysanthemums were stuck in her own jam jar. Plum, a boring jam. The wind thumped Viv's new panes like a fist. Joseph thought of delicate Oriental ghosts with faces like smashed porcelain and saw how the monk went on burning and undead Marilyn continued to laugh in the paper world of two dimensions where he himself now retreated, opening the book at random and diving into the shadowless print.

'I see nobody on the road,' said Alice.

'I only wish I had such eyes,' the king remarked in a fretful tone. 'To be able to see nobody. And at that distance, too!'

Shadows pursued him; they forced him to practise bibliomancy or divination by the book. He let it slither through his paws on to the floor. Miss Blossom, the husk of a woman, what was she doing? Making herself a small lunch of beans on toast or performing some other flat, thin activity, ironing rayon underwear or filling in a form? She kept the corners of her mouth well pressed in so as not to let anything escape. Or was she really Alice, had she seen him upstairs when nobody else could?

To his astonishment, when he drifted off to sleep, the cat securely back upon his pillow, he did not dream at all or if he did he dreamed of perfect blackness.

3

Joseph did not see Miss Blossom again until he was once more out and about and then it was in strange circumstances. His bandages were off, his scars healing but he was still shipwrecked in time; he went out very early one Sunday morning to buy some newspapers, which contained facts or, at least, accounts of things that might have happened. The sights and smells of the shop (crates of limeade, jars of barley sugar sticks and liquorice bootlaces, the tang of cardboard, newsprint and chocolate) were those of his earliest years and sometimes this trip was painfully nostalgic but mostly he felt perfectly indifferent. The newsagent was still sorting his stock as he drank tea from a pink mug. He was a heavy, cruel man, a former regular soldier; when he first saw Joseph's bandaged fingers, he said: 'Hello, I see you've been in the wars' with a curious relish. Joseph himself experienced a Gothic shudder to take newspapers and cigarettes from hands that had murdered in cold blood. The newsagent had a face the colour of offal.

Once Joseph was in the shop while Kay, in jungle-green forage cap, shades and ear-rings, was leafing through the paperback rack. He wore no shoes. His breathing was loud, noisy, moist and intimate; he giggled and spluttered over *Confessions of a Nymphomaniac, Secret Techniques of Erotic Delight* and a variety of translations from the Sanskrit while the newsagent eyed him up and down and slowly swelled with rage. He muttered: 'See that chap with the bare feet, God, I'd love to get him square bashing, those bare feet, one, two, jump to it, left, right.' But it was not really his clothes nor the length of his hair but a quality in Kay's essential texture, his curious radiance, the quality which affected Joseph with such indignation, that made him a walking affront to so many people.

Squaring his shoulders for an imaginary parade and drill, the newsagent announced it was a lovely morning. His thumb jabbed a screaming headline, the violation and murder of a child. There was a picture of the nondescript, middle-aged man convicted of the crime; he looked not unlike Joseph's father so he examined the caption carefully to make sure for you never could tell when the middle-aged might fly off the handle. The little girl was six years old and wore a heartbreaking ribbon in her hair.

'Flog 'em to death, that's what they should do to child murderers. Worse than animals. Flog them alive. I'd volunteer. Teach 'em a lesson.'

He took a noisy draft of tea and sold Joseph the *Observer*. Joseph, brooding about this violent start to the day, walked back the way he had come. It was by now the cold beginnings of winter. Frost rimed underfoot and blancoed the pipings of moss between the paving stones. In front of the crescent was a garden closed in iron railings. Here horse chestnuts and copper beeches were tearing off their leaves where once starched nannies watched scrubbed children play on a green baize lawn but now tramps slept in the abandoned potting-shed, the grass was long and rank and the only touch of elegance which remained was a small stone boy on a plinth playing a chipped stone whistle beside a spiky tangle of rose bushes; one of his arms had been carried away in the storm of years and rude messages of offensive lust scribbled across his belly. Today he wore a circumcision cap of frost, presiding over sad overgrown beds of fog-coloured Michaelmas daisies and brown undergrowth the colour of old photographs. He could have been the last of the lost children who, frozen by a whim of time before he could get out, remained there in stone perpetually harking to dead voices. Beyond the wild garden, the hill tipped down to the river where an immense golden fleece hung in the air; the sky was enamelled blue and gold, it was going to be a cold, glowing, beautiful day.

In the still, enchanted light the leprous walls of the crescent shone like the new Jerusalem, and since it was the day of rest, everybody was sweetly sleeping, cheeks on hands, heads on pillows, lovers, children and married couples, lost in blessed dreams, the old lady on the ground floor of Joseph's house dreaming of her father, herself the figurehead of his ship, breasting the waves of the limitless Pacific, Joseph's cat dreaming in the warm hollow of his mattress of unbelievably stupid pigeons and wings of children dropping from a cloud. Only in the garden something was not sleeping. Joseph stopped to look. In the gelid apricot morning, a ripple of movement made the debris of leaves and bushes tremble.

It was no dream. Perhaps it was a tramp risen from a bed of leaves and grass giving some orisons of curses to the new day. Or phantoms of Victorian children playing ghostly tig. Or Charlotte moving around beside the statue, some ghost in grey flannel moving around in the garden looking for something. Charlotte looking for something lost for ever, such as sentiment. Her heart. His heart. He saw the hard shoulders of an old-fashioned grey flannel suit such as Charlotte would never have worn only of course it was not Charlotte, anyway; she was in Hampstead, no doubt in bed with some Jew or Negro. This girl's hair blended with the tangled browns around her. It was Miss Blossom, alone and palely loitering. Miss A. Blossom, whose custard dish he had forgotten to return and never remembered to throw away her chrysanthemums, either, although they were quite dead. What could she be doing out in the garden so early in the morning? No birds sang. It was a mystery, she in her secretary suit among the withered flowers.

His curiosity aroused, Joseph crept down the stone stairs to the garden and peered through the railings. Built as it was on the side of a hill, the garden fell steeply away from itself in a ha-ha so that the lower branches of trees planted on the farther side spread at about shoulder height near the shed. Only a very few, lacy thin leaves were left on the branches. Miss Blossom held some branches in her arms, caressing the bony twigs with a blind lust, feverishly clutching them and stroking them. Her face was perfectly expressionless. Bells began to ring in a church somewhere. The morning was golden and quickly drying up the frost on the grass. In her stiff suit, Miss Blossom caressed the twigs where, just visible, just tangible, began to swell intimations of next year's leaves. Her eyes were blind and blank like those of the stone boy. Joseph was astonished she should have so much passion.

She was the quietest of women. She lived in the same house as he in complete obscurity. He never heard the sound of a radio or a record player from her room or the doorbell ringing for her. He never found her in the kitchen when he was using it. She moved in a fog of anonymity which obscured her completely. Nobody ever visited her. Sometimes letters for her lay on the table in the hall but either they came On Her Majesty's Service or they were impersonal circulars with three-penny stamps, never letters addressed in loopy script and violet ink or spiky pencil printing of children's hands nor birthday cards nor lumpy parcels. She raised her face blindly to the sun and embraced the living foliage like the tenderest of lovers. Time passed. The bells ceased to whirr and clamour and settled down to a steady single toll. Joseph knew he should not prey on this strange dryad who looked like a Dutch doll so he went home, made a small breakfast and, afterwards, tore up the *Observer* and made a number of paper aeroplanes. Sitting on the parapet outside his window and launching these aeroplanes on to the currents of the air, disseminating facts upon the wind, he thought all the time about Miss Blossom, but when he leaned out to look for her, either the branches screened her or she was gone.

But he was interested to hear a voice in his mind say sternly: 'Take her dish back, you thoughtless fellow!' After a little thought, he identified the voice as that of his superego. He was pleased to think his superego was still functioning; he feared he had mislaid it on his journey through the grave, if not before. It was a manly and decisive voice. He pictured its owner, Amazing Superego, a superhero such as Batman, Green Lantern or Captain America, a smooth-crotched giant in white tights with a silver helmet on his head. The villain would be Idman, a slimy, writhing, green and mauve riot of Art Nouveau swirls. Superego versus Idman. Pity the poor ego in between the battle. He obeyed the voice; he decided to take her dish back. Therefore he combed his hair and tidied himself a little.

He was very dirty and unkempt. There was a grey spray of stubble over his face which was still covered in scabs. His hair had grown over his greasy shirt collar. Looking at his fractured image in the glass, it occurred to him he could easily give up completely and end his days like old Sunny or worse, without even the comfort of an imaginary violin. His hair was tangled almost into felt and his hands were very clumsy with disuse. He hoped she was a maternal woman and would maybe offer to wash his shirts but, as it turned out, she was not at home. It had taken so much effort and mental turmoil to make the brief descent to her door (he had even washed her Pyrex bowl in the kitchen and dried it, too) that he was full of affront when there was no answer to his knock. He shook his fist at the door where a tacked notice in plump, copybook capitals read simply: BLOSSOM. He did not know what time it was; it could have been morning church time or even afternoon walk time. He tried to guess where she could have gone but could think of nowhere. He hammered at the door in impotent fury but when he tried the handle he found it opened immediately for she was unsuspicious and had nothing to hide or worth stealing.

BLOSSOM. He stepped into her room, which was larger than his attic but, since it was at the back of the house, had no view except the flat top of a supermarket. There was not even enough room in the view for a fair-sized piece of sky. The walls were papered with silvery faded lavender floral stripes; there was a border of wisteria. This room never caught the sun. It was a furnished room and full of landlord's furniture – a narrow, lumpy bed, a brown-stained dressing-table with ill-fitting drawers, a rickety gate-leg table. He was glad he lived among his own honest orange boxes and sticks with none of the junk that filled the rest of the house.

Miss Blossom had made no attempt to alter or transform the room except to place a small pottery squirrel and a pink enamel alarm clock on the mantelpiece, beneath a red cabbage and gravy picture of cattle in a Highland stream, obviously the landlord's taste. In the silence, the clock's little tick was overbusy, a small unpleasantness like the buzzing of a fly. The hands stood at ten to three. Three nylon stockings hung to dry from a coat hanger suspended in the fireplace. There was a built-in cupboard. He opened the door. Cups and plates. A twin for the Pyrex bowl.

On another shelf some cosmetics, cold cream and rachel face powder and a lipstick. He fumbled this open and tried the colour on his wrist. It was extremely pink. She had tied up a stack of women's magazines carefully with string ready for the waste-paper collector. Hardly anything in her cupboard or her room showed she could exist with the vividness of the ugly Eve he had seen in the garden that morning.

He put the bowl he carried down on the gate-leg table, which shivered under the impact. The room contained nothing but a musty female smell, sweetish and old. Miss Blossom wore a heavy veil over her personality. Joseph pulled open a drawer in her dressing-table and found nothing but underwear, some serviceable cotton bras, knickers and slips. A home-perm kit in its cardboard box. Nothing else. He did not know what he had expected to find, perhaps a little oak tree in a pot or the crimson heart out of her bosom tucked away for safety in a handkerchief sachet.

Then he caught sight of himself in the mirror and was transfixed. Mirror, mirror on the wall, who is the ugliest of them all. He had not seen himself in a three-quarters mirror for months and now discovered himself wrist deep in lingerie. Walt Whiteman on a pantie prowl or Don Quixote indulging in a subterranean fetish, there he was, scarred, stubbled and coiffed like a patriarch of the Old Believers, gaunt as famine, filthy and dishevelled when he had done his best to tidy himself, fingering this unknown girl's private garments with his repulsive hands. He was ashamed. He shut the drawer as quickly as the warped, swollen wood let him but the action of shutting the difficult drawer set a little celluloid box on top of the dressing-table rattling like a seed-filled gourd. It was a round box with a bunny rabbit in low relief on the lid, possibly intended as a receptacle for safety pins for babies. It was old, dented and discoloured and contained two relics of the oldest story in the world; a tiny curl of exceedingly fine and silky hair tied with a scrap of blue ribbon and a slim gold engagement ring with a single chip of diamond stone in it, the cheapest kind. Joseph recalled how, after the Dresden fire raids, they collected all the rings in buckets to identify the victims from their inscriptions of love. Very gently, he replaced the lid on the celluloid box and left the room, closing the door softly behind him as if he did not want to disturb somebody.

So Miss Blossom's was a modest history of love and betrayal, as commonplace and overwhelming a tragedy as each of the road accident statistics or any girl crying softly into her pillow so as not to wake her mother or husband or the administration of terminal drugs of comfort and hopelessness; scrawny, pinched, virginal Miss Blossom was sadly abandoned to ill fortune like the stone boy on his plinth, in a perpetual October. Awake but dreaming of simple domestic misfortunes such as hare lips, skin diseases and impotence, Joseph lay on his mattress and watched the first stars appear in his window; Viv sprang in, exploding the room with light. He wanted Joseph to come out for a drink with his mother, who was free tonight.

'Here, though you aren't half in a mess. All hair and dirt. You aren't half letting yourself go, you're as bad as when they threw you out of the college of knowledge. You need a good dose of soap and water, that's what you need.'

Viv himself shone with soap and water. His monkey hair was spickly parted in the mathematical centre and his Kaiser Wilhelm moustache most beautifully combed. He was casually dressed in ex-naval bellbottoms which had cost him seven shillings and sixpence and a lilac wool sweater which once belonged to his mother; his self-possession was so great and his genial smile so continuous he gave the impression of total propriety and exquisite taste. He walked like a man in a solid gold hat. Joseph permitted Viv to brush him down for he was covered with biscuit crumbs, which formed a thick sediment in the bed, but there was no time to wash and he bitterly regretted his dirty face when he saw Mrs Boulder for she was, as always, immaculate.

She was sitting by herself on a leather bench of the brown-panelled, chintz-curtained lounge bar of a big, bleak, red-brick pub on the riverside road. There was no one else in the bar. In an alcove behind her head was an arrangement of plastic tulips and daffodils, lit by neon strip. She was drinking whisky and light ale. She was uneasy to be alone and watched the door nervously. Her hands clutched so tightly on the gild chain handle of her white quilted shiny handbag that the white kid of her gloves was stretched smooth and shiny over her knuckles. She was spotless in a white woollen suit; her jacket was so tight the seaming of her brassiere was visible because she did not wear a blouse. A shiny white raincoat was neatly folded on the seat beside her. She was fat, white and painted like a holy statue.

'God, Joseph, you look awful,' she said. She had a London accent and did not speak often although her voice was beautifully dark and cool. She never told Joseph what part of London she came from nor asked any questions or volunteered any information. He kissed her enamel cheek. Her terrifying naked eyes had grown no older, were still thirty years younger than she and now were full of solicitude and pure motherly care. He remembered how he thought she had kissed him but knew it had been a dream or she very, very drunk.

'You look like a tramp,' she said with despair for she believed that clothes make the man. She gave Viv a pound note and told him to buy them drinks; then she became quite silent and sipped her whisky, crooking her little finger in a ladylike way that Viv copied, leaving a thick heart of lipstick on the rim of her glass. Joseph felt a wave of affection.

'What a frost we had this morning,' he said; they always had formal weather conversations and sometimes health conversations.

'It's only to be expected for the time of year,' said Viv, who was far less boisterous in his mother's presence for he knew how much she loved him and this oppressed him a little. Mrs Boulder lowered her huge eyelids, the colour and shape of mussel shells.

'Summertime is over for good,' she said in an expressionless voice which nevertheless carried deep blue hints of poignant symbolic overtones.

'I see they put the clocks back,' said Viv with obscure content.

Joseph sighed with reassurance. There was a strict precision like that of a baroque recorder ensemble in conversation with mother and son; enormously long, harmonious silences were part of the score. During these silences, the battering winds lulled and the flames parted to let through the victims unharmed. She took a packet of mentholated King Size cigarettes from the perfumed interior of her handbag; they always smoked her cigarettes. Her handbag clunked when she shifted it because it was full of lipsticks, gilt powder compacts, boxes of rouge and eye shadow kits. She began to look intently at something in the mirror behind the bar, something ugly but quite absorbing which Viv and Joseph would never see. They were quite snug in the little brown room; nobody else came in and the barman spent most of his time chatting with friends in the public bar.

'Get some more drinks, Vivvy.'

Joseph had a little money but she ignored him and crackled across another pound to her son.

'After all,' she said, 'it's easy come, easy go.'

'What did you say that girl's name was, Viv?'

'What girl?'

'The one who found me.'

'Oh. Anne. Orphan Annie.'

'She –' but why should he tell his friends the secrets of a perfect stranger? He stopped short. 'Nothing.'

'I see her carrying her typewriter,' said Viv vaguely.

'When?'

'On buses about five thirtyish. When you'd expect.'

'Of course, you travel on buses a lot and so on.'

'Want some crisps?' Mum? Joseph?'

'No. No thanks.'

'Mum? Mum! Want some crisps?'

She wore a plain gilt cross on a slender chain dangling way down the deep vee of swelling amber flesh between the lapels of her jacket. This gentle, withered skin was the true covering of her abused flesh, down below the lowest peachy tidemarks of base and powder. Viv sucked at those breasts in his simian babyhood. Viv now neatly nibbling one by one through the salt 'n' vinegar flavour crisps he had bought with her money.

'Is the Electric Opera doing well?'

'So so. The stroboscope broke down last night. I nearly had a fit.'

Joseph went through the public bar to the lavatory. The public bar was quite different to the lounge bar; it was far larger, far colder, no snug carpet underfoot but chilly, clinking tiles. There was a fruit machine; a young boy in jeans and a leather jacket on the back of which the words 'Drag City' were picked out in gilded studs desultorily played it. The scars on the leather benches around the walls looked as if made with knives. In the empty grate were squashed cigarette packets and a fresh gob of sputum. Two old ladies in grey knitted cardigans peered up at Joseph and then commenced to sip their brown ale and murmur in perturbation as if his appearance portended the end of the world. A young boy with a narrow, pale face and an upstanding crest of greased black hair operated the juke box. The robot arm extended and selected a piece of rock and roll. A young man and a girl sat at a round table. The girl had extraordinary flashing black eyes and a backcombed beehive of black hair; she seemed all vitality but the young man was pale and listless. His navy-blue suit was too sharp. His tie was pink. His hair was curling and dark gold. They held hands. The bar was bleak but peaceful; but when Joseph came out again, everything was changed.

Kay used this pub occasionally. He had come in; the music was over.

The black-eyed girl was on her feet, doing a fandango; she began to punch holes in the disquieting silence with bursts of metallic laughter and clicked her fingers as if they were castanets. It was a mating dance display and yet it had the freezing menace of a dance in an Elizabethan tragedy performed by disguised assassins concealing knives. Abruptly she broke off and, with a strange maternal gesture, turned to cradle the head of the young man in the pink tie to her heaving breast. He seemed content to play a passive prop in this scene she was acting. The old ladies huddled and murmured. Kay picked his nose. The boy with the pink tie had taxidermy eyes like a dead, stuffed deer; if you looked long enough into his eyes, you would start screaming. Joseph began to feel an intense concern for him, with his dead eyes. The girl kissed his tousled curls but kept on looking at Kay, who seemed smaller than ever in the open spaces of the public bar.

'I wasn't doing anything, just buying ciggies, and she threw a glass at me before I got my change,' he said as if to himself, in a tone of infinite regret.

This glass lay in pieces on the floor. The pub dog, a plump, ageing fox terrier, bounced right up in the air, all four feet off the ground, whining, anxious to see over the bar. A pale spectre appeared in the doorway, Mrs Boulder.

'You started it, you rotten fairy!' stated the girl emphatically. Her eyes flashed, her bosom rocked up and down. 'You started it so I threw a glass at you.'

There was a jagged atmosphere in the bar; things were happening without a sequence, there was no flow or pattern to events. Causation was still awry. Violence seemed suspended in the air, about to happen.

'It is a world of troubles,' said the barman gnomically.

The boy in the pink tie suddenly twisted together with a jerk and spoke. He reminded Joseph of somebody. He spoke very quickly, in a confused babble.

'Her mother's Irish, I can't control an Irish temper, she's got a temper like fire, her mother's Irish, she's half Mick, how do you expect me to control an Irish temper – I can't control an Irish temper –'

'I can see that,' said Kay with some asperity. He said to the barman in a pained voice, 'I've never made trouble in this pub or acted in an anti-social way and then some lunatic lobs a glass at me, it's not good enough, you know, letting in lunatics like –'

But before he could say any more, the boy in the pink tie gave a sharp, high-pitched cry and lunged forward. He flew through the air; immediately, with an elegant flourish and an air of the flying ballet, Kay leapt up on to the bar. Missing his target, the other crashed down upon the floor among the smashed glass. Kay stood on the bar top and looked down impassively. The old ladies at the other end of the bar decided to sip their brown ale as if nothing was happening. The dog began to bark loudly. The boy in the pink tie writhed and sobbed on the tiles. He spilled out more words.

'I can't control an Irish temper and she's always looked after me, I'm three parts mental. I'm just out of a mental hospital and I'm three parts mental, don't call me a lunatic for Christ's sake, and there you are in your golden ear-rings and I'm looking at you, what you want to wear golden ear-rings for if you don't want to be looked at, I'm looking at you peacefully and you say "What's with you, friend," and I can't bear it, it's too much —'

The girl stood with her hands on her hips; her demonic red lips were stretched in a flamenco dancer's artificial smile.

'It's not true,' she said. 'He's just out of the nick. God, what a liar he is.'

The boy rolled in the dirt, a filthy fountain of tears. Kay took off his shades and polished them. He had wide, cool, pale eyes; without his sunglasses, he showed a bland, even sweet face. He put on his shades again; now he looked like the Demon King.

'He should get himself a new bird,' he stated in a voice like a windbell. The girl drew a sharp breath, picked up another glass from a table and threw it at Kay; it missed him and shattered against the bar, cracking a bottle of gin which burst out in a blue-white waterfall. The dog went on barking and Kay departed from the bar via a stool as swiftly as a bird or Peter Pan on a wire from above. Then there was only broken glass and tears in the bar and the old ladies suddenly talking more loudly. The youth with the black crest slid another sixpence into the juke box and the resident of Drag City picked his way through the splinters to buy a shandy and Joseph realized the boy with the pink tie reminded him of the badger in the zoo, the mad badger, stuffed and trapped in the final humiliation of a glass cage but still insanely crying 'No surrender' against an insane world. He went to help him to his feet but the girl got there first. She knelt down and caressed the weeper fiercely. He raised a face streaked black and white with tears.

'I'd have killed him,' he said. 'I'd have strangled him with my bare hands, given a little time.'

She sat back on her heels and began to laugh with whole-hearted, full-throated derision, very ugly to hear. She laughed until the paint around her eyes began to smudge.

'You'll be the death of me,' she said. 'You and your fucking party tricks.'

In the lounge bar, Mrs Boulder was a quaking, shaking, melting snow-woman. Viv poured her back into her coat.

'That cut-price Magnani next door!' exclaimed Viv. 'Trying to send her poor bloke off his twist like that!'

'I hate violence,' said Mrs Boulder. 'How I hate violence. Oh, Vivvy, oh, my heart. I can't bear violence.'

They got her into the street and thence home.

'I'm all aflutter,' she said. 'I'll go to bed.'

'Coming up for a bit, my lover?' invited Viv. 'We could watch the telly,' he added palely.

'No,' said Joseph, gripped by a fever. 'No, but would you have a pair of wire-cutters in the house to lend me and perhaps a sack?'

'There are the wire-cutters from when I tuned the piano,' said Viv doubtfully. 'But whatever do you want wire-cutters for?'

'I'm going to set the badger free,' said Joseph, dancing with impatience, for he knew it was the most important thing in the world.

Viv was full of misgivings but at last found the cutters for Joseph; there was no sack in the flat but he lent Joseph a zipped hold-all which would be large enough to contain the badger.

'I'd come with you but I can't leave the old lady, can I,' he said, his loyalties torn. She was lying on her generous bed and groaning so loudly she could be heard in the tiny hall. Joseph, utterly preoccupied, snatched bag and cutters with some mutters of thanks and hurried off. Overhead, a round, puss-faced moon smiled down.

Joseph ran up the hill; he ran, breathless, up the lane behind the rotting crescent where Kay lived, all the balconies overlooking the city: debouching from this alleyway in darkness lit only by a few old-fashioned gas lamps and a little treacherous moonlight, he sprang into the road. Kay, approaching on his bicycle, rang his bell with passion, clenched his brakes, made contact and tumbled off. The bicycle keeled over. There was a confusion of whirling wheels and some twanging noises like plucked fiddle strings. Kay sat on the ground. His very thin arms and legs stuck out at strange angles, like those of a stick insect. Joseph halted, gasping, bewildered at this interruption.

'More haste, less speed,' said Kay after a while. It was remarkable he managed to see anything with his dark glasses on.

'I always think of cyclists as being perfectly mechanically self-sufficient,' said Joseph, looking with something of wonder at this prone mechanical centaur.

'Give us a hand up, you thoughtless thing,' said Kay. His hand felt light, dry, thin and insubstantial.

'Where were you going so quickly?' he asked when he was on his feet again and adjusting the padded combat jacket he wore, which seemed to have protected him from injury.

'I'm going to set the badger free,' explained Joseph.

Kay scratched his car.

'What, from the zoo? Let out poor Brock?'

'Yes. I have some wire-cutters with me to snip a hole in his cage.'

Kay picked up the bicycle and shook it to see if anything fell off; nothing did.

'Many hands make light work,' he said and fell into step beside Joseph, wheeling his bicycle. They progressed this way in perfect silence up the elegant main street, crossed the road beside the coffee shop and struck across the wide, undulating Down, which was a huge expanse of common land tended at the edges, where the Obelisk was, but lonely and wild in the middle regions. The zoo lay on the other side, over on the far edge of the Down. The night was full of autumn smells, mist, frost, mushrooms. It was very cold and the eerie moonlight played tricks with moving shadows. After a while, Kay began to whistle some tunes; first he whistled, 'Dance, dance, dance, little lady', and then he whistled 'On the Good Ship Lollipop'. Joseph thought only of the badger going round and round and round in its cage, in and out of labyrinthine patterns cast by moonlit wire netting.

They ploughed on through knee-high grass. Gorse-bushes still dotted with blossom and briars horny with berries, all bleached to constructions of bones in the moonlight, snatched and tore at their flesh and clothing. Kay began to whistle 'Limehouse Blues' and after he finished it was silent until they came to the high, grim, back wall of the zoo and they stood in its shadow under the moon, gazing up at it. Kay looked inquiringly at Joseph to see what he would do next but Joseph was searching for footholds and handholds in the wall, which was smooth as glass.

'Here,' said Kay, propping his bicycle against the wall. He set one foot upon the saddle and in an instant crouched precariously on the rough broken glass at the top, high above Joseph, silhouetted against the sky.

'There is a flowerbed on the other side,' he reported. 'What if the dahlias are staked, I've got a lot to lose, you know.' Then he sighed. 'Still, in for a penny, in for a pound, I suppose.'

He jumped to the earth. Joseph heard a soft thud and a few muffled exclamations; he tossed the hold-all over the wall and followed by Kay's method. He was entirely consumed by the urgency of his quest and made a soft landing among crushed plants where Kay stood rubbing a bruised arm and muttering some small whimpering complaints to himself. Joseph retrieved the hold-all.

'Over there,' he said. 'Next to the gibbons.'

Now he ran in earnest, fleeing across the zoo like rain before the wind, and Kay followed. Both wore rubber shoes and made no sound. All the denizens of the zoo were locked in animal sleeps of jungle, tundra or polar wastes: deer and wallaby fastened for the night in wooden chalets; monkeys in close odorous indoors scratching for fleas in their sleep; elephants, what kind of philosophies did elephants dream? Shadows of cages in the moonlight made intricate traps on paths and lawns; the pond where the waterbirds swam was sleepy black as Lethe. They arrived at the cage of the poor badger. Habitat British Isles, he was hardened to the weather and, fortunately for them, he slept outdoors in a straw-filled kennel. Joseph and Kay stood staring through the mesh at the hole behind which the badger slept. Only then, within sight of his goal, as he regained his breath, did Joseph's obsession loosen its grip enough for him to fully perceive his companion.

'Jesus, it's Kay Kyte,' he said, full of revulsion to taste in his mouth the names of birds of prey. 'Go away and dine with your kind, the vultures, Kay Kyte.'

'What a rotten thing to say,' said Kay in a small, hurt voice. 'You'd never have got over that wall if it wasn't for me and then you go and say a horrible thing like that.'

Although Joseph was not a tall man, Kay's head in the khaki forage cap scarcely reached to his shoulder but this did not make him feel magnanimous and protective towards Kay. However, he shrugged his shoulders and began to cut a hole in the wire netting big enough to step through.

'Watch out the badger doesn't wake and bolt,' he warned. 'He'd only go to earth somewhere in the zoo and never be free.'

Kay's shades purely reflected the moon, as if he had large silver eyelids; he crept very close to Joseph, eagerly watching the work. Joseph felt his moist breath on his bent neck and his wrists, Kay's curious breathing like that of a small child or wild animal. Somehow his breathing seemed a very intimate thing which he performed in public with a certain self-consciousness. His presence was warm and smelled of sweat and incense.

After a while, Kay said in a dreamy voice: 'What lovely strong hands you have, Joseph.'

Joseph was very annoyed.

'Cool it or piss off,' he snapped.

Joseph was grateful for Kay's help but very much wished he hadn't run into him for, besides the complicated mixture of envy, resentment and distaste he felt for the little man, he also guessed Kay would somehow manage to grab all the credit for this important rescue and it would become another of Kay's legendary exploits. These thoughts flashed on to various screens in small sideshows of his mind but the main theatre was so busy with the escape itself, the actual penetration of the cage, he had not time to remonstrate with Kay for choosing this moment to attempt a pass. With every moment's work, his hands were regaining their old cunning.

Still the badger slept in its box. No nocturnal animal pressed luminescent eyes against the bars of any near-by cage to see what they were doing. Snip, snip, went the wire-cutters. There were no sounds in the universe but those of Kay's breathing and the teeth of the wire-cutters gnashing together, biting through metal, and there was no world outside these shapes of trees, cages and ornamental shrubs; the zoo itself was striped black and white with shadows and moonlight like a huge badger dead and lying upon the ground. Joseph began to feel dizzy and exalted, drugged. When the hole was big enough, he stepped into the enclosure, although it took him all his courage to voluntarily step into a cage. Kay followed him and looked around with interest: a pleased smile suddenly descended on his whimsical features for this was something new and he thrived on novelties but Joseph was trembling with both a kind of ecstasy and a fear of imprisonment.

'I tried to clip my way out of the cage of flesh but had a spectacular failure,' he said suddenly.

'I'm sure we shall do better with Brock,' responded Kay in a comfortable voice. He knelt beside the badger's box bed.

'Come out badger,' he said. 'We're all friends here.'

Joseph knelt down on the other side.

'Hello, little Brock,' he said. 'The weather's lovely.'

The badger poked forth a questing nose. With a subdued howl of glee, Kay plunged his hands into the kennel, snatched out the animal and thrust it bodily into the hold-all, slamming down the zip. It was all over in a moment. The hold-all commenced to jump up and down, whickering very loudly.

'What appalling violence,' said Joseph. 'Just what I would expect from a bird of prey, you kyte.'

'You've got to be cruel to be kind,' observed Kay. Then adopting a 'B' feature film American accent: 'C'mon, baby, let's blow this place.'

He humped the rearing, jumping hold-all and they passed back through the man-shaped opening in the netting and sprinted down the silvery paths until Joseph saw a ladder propped against the side of a greenhouse; so they returned over the wall more easily than they had come and found themselves out in the Down again, among the whispering bushes.

'What shall we do with Brock?' asked Kay in a worried voice.

'We shall let him out and he'll dig himself a hole,' said Joseph. 'That is the nature of badgers.'

But the badger solved the problem by itself. While they stood undecided, it completed gnawing through a corner of the hold-all and plopped out on to the grass. It was gone in a flash. The undergrowth rustled. Then no more. Joseph was full of joy. He took the destroyed hold-all from Kay. The badger would frisk on the grass beneath the moon, taste dew of morning, plunge into the earth again.

'Will it find food?' asked Kay suddenly. 'If it runs out on to the main road, will it be killed?'

'Whatever happens to it, at least it is free,' said Joseph.

'I see you set considerable store by that,' said Kay.

'Well, yes. I suppose I do,' said Joseph.

'Well, I hope it will be all right, that's all, after all we've done.' Kay gave a little sigh as if uncertain that they had done the right thing, after all. 'I shall go and find my bike,' he said and wandered off without another word, although he began to whistle 'Pedro the Fisherman'. The night soon swallowed him up although the spoor of his whistle lingered in the air for a long time and Joseph set off home alone. Kay's doubts made him uneasy; his joy evaporated. It would be ironic to set the badger free only to have it die the same night under the wheels of a car. He felt empty, unsure.

Then, coming upon a bushy hollow, he saw the glimmer of fire. It was a rubbishy fire of sticks and papers. Around it sat three old men in ultimate rags and filth. An operatic trick of the firelight made their faces seem grotesque masks of sores and wrinkles hanging in the air. They drank together in a communion of despair; maybe one that night would roll into the embers of the fire as he slept, to burn and smoulder like wood, not flesh, as if the ravaged substance had itself atrophied.

4

Ransome's room was painted cream and green; he had a piece of nasty carpet on his dark-blue linoleum floor and a scratched wooden desk with a maroon leatherette top. He sat in a furry grey armchair on one side of this desk while Joseph sat on a tubular steel stacking chair with a seat of khaki canvas on the other side; his face was half hidden by the upturned collar of his coat. Sometimes, to bridge the gap or bring Joseph out of hiding, Ransome tried an anecdote.

'The police rang us up the other day, they were in a frightful tizzy. "Come at once," they said, "we've got a most peculiar transvestite in the station"; I said, "Tell me something new, you're always pulling in transvestites these days", and they replied, "You don't understand, he's not a normal pervert ..."' His voice trailed away when he saw the Jacobean leer with which Joseph regarded him.

'What would you say if I told you I'd desecrated a church?' confided Joseph through twisted lips.

'I'd remind you Shelley's dead,' said Ransome. 'Byron, too.' Joseph was delighted.

'I'd never have dreamed you were sophisticated enough to have said that,' he remarked almost admiringly.

'Don't underestimate me, Joseph,' said Ransom with such an undertone of menace Joseph started; they exchanged the long, hooded glance of chess masters in a grand tournament until Joseph escaped into privacy by covering his face with his hands.

'Speaking of dreams, how are your nights?' inquired Ransome in his normal voice.

'It's a three-ring circus the moment I close my eyes. Last night, amongst other things, I dreamed I was on an anvil in a forge under a mountain and three men in Gestapo uniform were making me into guns, knives and iron crosses. Then I wake up every morning to the odour of corruption, this disgusting reek of my body.'

'That might be more interesting if you were not so dirty,' said Ransome with perceptible distaste. 'What do you do with your Unemployment Benefit that you can't afford soap and water.'

Joseph looked furtively through his webbed fingers. He was still randomly distributing among meths drinkers and rag pickers the few shillings left after his rent and a little food were paid for but he knew already that Ransome interpreted these charities as pathological indications.

'If I had a great deal of money,' he said, cunningly side-tracking the psychiatrist, 'I'd sail around the world in a yacht with a sycophant or two, I guess you know where you are with sycophants. And I'd buy some corrupt psychiatrists for my very own, not make do with the sparse integrity of the National Health Service. Also, I would open a gallery displaying pictures of famous assassins.'

'You are beginning to look like an assassin,' said Ransome. 'You look like John Wilkes Booth.'

'The actor who shot Lincoln; I saw him in *Birth of a Nation*,' said Joseph, 'Jesus, what a ham. Assassins should have a little dignity, if nobody else has.'

'I'd have thought you'd abhor assassination, with this hatred of violence you're always proclaiming,' suggested Ransome.

'Oh, I'm all for shooting politicians,' said Joseph. 'It's murder I can't stomach.'

'You make fine distinctions.'

'Not fine at all. I'll ask you a riddle: what is the difference between Lyndon Johnson and the Boston Strangler.'

'I give up,' said Ransome at once.

'One is an honest butcher,' said Joseph. 'Only I'm not sure which.'

Then he caught sight of Ransome stifling a yawn and demanded: 'Pardon my paranoia but am I boring you? Say if I'm boring you and I'll shut up, the worst thing in the world would be to bore one's psychiatrist.'

By now he could have drawn a map of Ransome's face, the light wrinkles, the bland, colourless cheeks, the dints left either side of the nose from the pressure of his spectacles. No hurricane ever tore across these cool prairies nor furious winter's rages blasted the smooth promontories of nose and chin; Ransome controlled his weather like the Iceland witches who keep the winds in a leather bag. Joseph felt he would have to take his shoes off if he wanted to walk across Ransome's face for it was sanctified ground. And yet he possessed many quicksands and traps for Joseph; now he smiled.

'A good deal of your sickness is merely a failure to adjust to the twentieth century,' he said. Joseph could hardly believe his ears.

'You're not a man, you're a cliché,' he snarled viciously, showing all his teeth, which were beginning to rot.

'Let's take the Vietnam war,' Ransome went on. 'I don't think you care at all about the sufferings of the people of Vietnam, Joseph; not in any real sense of involvement with a real situation. You make no move to relieve those sufferings in a real way, through voluntary service, for example. You don't even join in any organized protest. Rather, you've taken this dreadful tragedy of war as a symbolic event and you draw a simple melodramatic conclusion from this complex tragedy — you use it as a symbol for your rejection of a world to which you cannot relate. Perhaps because of your immaturity.'

He took off his glasses and wiped them; at once his face became less oracular and more human, weary. His colourless eyes hung in nets of tired lines, like trawled fish.

'You're a bad actor, Joseph, just as Booth was, and not even a conscientious one, just like him. You've read nothing of the play but your own lines. Booth if you remember, just managed to mouth out: *"Sic semper tyrannis"*.'

'And then he died,' said Joseph. Ransome shrugged. There was a moment's silence. The heatpipes coughed. Then Joseph darted across the room to the sash window and threw it up. A violent inrush of wind set Ransome's papers aflutter. Joseph scrambled out on to the window ledge.

'Taunt me with lack of heart and I'll jump,' he said. 'What else can I do but make gestures? You're older than me. Tell me.'

They stared at each other. Ransome remained inscrutable: he donned his glasses once more and Joseph saw his double reflection gazing back at him from the lenses. His own face repeated twice was all the message he received. Ransome reassembled his scattered papers. In his mind's eye. Joseph saw little children clad in flame and the Mekong Delta like one gigantic wound.

'I'll jump for you,' he said.

'You're wedged in the gap between art and life,' said Ransome in a tired voice, as if nothing unusual had happened. He opened a drawer, found a stone and weighed his papers down with it. He scribbled something on a pad.

'Here's another prescription, Joseph,' he said. 'Try to get plenty of fresh air.'

He rose from his chair, nestled it neatly beneath his desk, smiled kindly at Joseph outside the window and left the room. Looking down, Joseph realized he perched only a couple of storeys above a small garden and so would have fallen soft, on grass, anyway. His angel was watching over him, he could hear its coarse laughter. He climbed back into the room and pocketed the prescription; he found a stub of pencil and wrote in very large letters on Ransome's pad: ANOTHER FORNICATING TRAN-QUILLIZER, I DON'T TRUST BASTARDS LIKE YOU, YOU BASTARD. He made a paper boat out of the prescription and floated it on the pond in the middle of the Down, pelting it with small pebbles until it sank.

Above his head, seagulls cried and circled in the clear, grey skies of early winter. The little pond lay in a grassy hollow far from the road. It was round like an eye. The water in the pond was grey and gritty as tears. Joseph remembered how Alice was afraid she might drown in the huge pool she had wept; he scooped up a handful of pond water and touched it with his tongue, discovering, as he had expected, a saline, brackish taste. Now it seemed to Joseph the earth itself was alive, bleeding and suffering, a perfectly sentient substance whose eyes were full of tears. He fell on his knees beside this weeping eye and plunged his arms into the chill, shallow water, grasping handfuls of pebbles and waterweed on the pond bottom as if they were tokens of essence. At length, prompted by mysterious intuitions, he rolled entirely into the pond and lay down full-length in water colder than he would have believed possible, lay still as a dead tree trunk, gnawing his lips to avoid shivering. Gulls tossed on the wind. His hair floated out upon the water like that of drowned Ophelia.

Then a large dog appeared on the horizon at a gallop, tongue lolling; it came rapidly down the slope and charged the pond. Joseph was overwhelmed with spray; when he could see and breathe properly again, the dog had seized a fold of his jacket between his teeth and was tugging it.

'Go away,' requested Joseph morosely. He recognized the dog as the one who stole Sunny's cap; he wore a collar with a name tag engraved 'Solly'. The dog began to wag its tail. Joseph, entirely saturated, got up from the water. He was plastered with weed and mud. The dog tugged and pulled at him, almost pulling him over.

'What's the scene, Solly?' said Joseph. 'What's on your mind?'

The dog let go of him and whined very loudly; it ran to the other side of the pond where it stood in a listening attitude, one paw raised as if beseeching Joseph to listen. Then back it splashed to Joseph and tugged again.

'Do you want me to come with you? Is that it?'

Solly wagged his tail so enthusiastically an arc of water sprayed across the pool. He grinned and panted. Joseph allowed the dog to lead him over the desolate wastes of Down, where perhaps the badger was excavating a set under the ground, he could only hope so; they came to a brown clump of gorse still pricked out with yellow flowers where, half hidden among these bushes, Miss Blossom lay on the scanty grass. The craggy undulations of her body were no more hospitable than the moorland which rolled around them. She lay with infinite propriety. Her skirt was pulled well down and her hands were neatly folded in front of her, resting on her handbag. She took in Joseph's extraordinary appearance at a glance.

'I see you've been abusing yourself again,' she said; her lips set in a hard line.'

The wolfish dog, its duty done, sat down plump with an air of self-satisfaction, fixing its dark, bright, intent eyes upon them. Joseph absently patted Solly's head. A spout of water jetted from his sleeve; he half-expected to see a minnow or two spill out and an S.O.S. in a bottle.

'The sedge is withered from the lake, Miss Blossom,' he said, combing waterweed and some sweet papers from his hair with his fingers.

'I was waiting for assistance,' said Miss Blossom, coldly.

'That big dog brought it, I mean, me,' said Joseph, who felt a little light-headed.

Solly thumped his tail against the ground with a dull, thudding noise like a distant tambourine.

'Help me to my feet,' she said although she examined his wet and filthy hands and arms with unease. But she was forced, nevertheless, to accept their aid to raise herself upright. Accidentally they found themselves gazing deeply into each other's eyes but no flashes of recognition passed between her opaque and his hollow regard. The top of her frizzy perm brushed his cheek. Holding on to him she set her right foot hard on the ground, winced and caught her breath in a sob.

'My ankle is sprained or twisted,' she said.

'How did you fall?'

'The dog chased me. I didn't know it was a friendly dog. I saw some wild animal galloping through the bushes and that frightened me. You don't expect wild animals and things in the middle of the city. And then the dog came out of the blue and chased me and I tripped among the roots of the gorse bushes because I'm not the best runner in the world, with this limp of mine.'

It was a long speech; she was obviously angry to have to recite it.

'Lean on me and keep the weight off your bad ankle,' said Joseph. She picked up her square handbag and, gingerly clasping Joseph's arm with the tips of her fingers, eased herself forward but stumbled and gave a little shriek.

'You'll have to lean on me more closely than that,' said Joseph. 'Everyone has to trust a stranger some time, you know.'

'Oh, it's not that,' she said, dismissing trust. 'Only, honest, you don't half look unsavoury, you look like they'd dragged you up and out of a canal or something. It's horrible to touch you.'

'Come on, come on,' said Joseph, who appreciated how she felt.

Reluctantly she had at last to lie as close as any bride against his shoulder and they began to make some progress. The dog followed them. His identity disc tinkled like a little bell. Miss Blossom's face was so near to Joseph he could see the photogravure grain of her skin beneath the deposits of powder and smell her body smell, a sad, sour smell of yesterday's reawakened sweat and labour; she was a working girl.

They walked in the grey cloud of her indifference until:

'I went for a walk, see,' she volunteered abruptly. 'There is so much of the Down and it is so nice to feel you're in the country although it is still the city, so to speak. So I fancied a breath of air. Who'd have thought there'd be all these wild animals?'

Why should a cripple go walking for pleasure? Her face was all locked up.

'You do seem a mystery to me.'

'I am a perfectly ordinary girl.' After a time, she said: 'Why is that 'orrible dog padding along behind us like that, it gives me the creeps.'

'Maybe he is a police dog,' said Joseph with a pastel-tinted humour. The dog wagged his tail good naturedly to show he could take a joke but Miss Blossom, Anne – Joseph remembered her name was Anne – said, 'Well, I wish it wouldn't tag along, that's all.'

'He only wants to make friends.'

'That was why it knocked me down, was it, to make friends. I don't want to be friends with no dogs.'

'The animal you say, tell me, was it black and white? Was it a badger and did it look free?'

'I saw it running. It scared me. I didn't want to look close, did I, I'm not a fool, it could have bit me.'

'I see.'

In this way, they reached the Obelisk at last. No children played. It was about three o'clock, the dead middle of the afternoon. Joseph looked down and saw granules of dandruff lying against hair as dry as old newspapers but though her skin and hair were rough she was unmistakably youthful at close quarters, she could be no more than twenty-five, perhaps younger, perhaps his own age. She leaned against him, resting, at the roadside, watching the cars go by. The weather had changed as they walked; the sky was now harsh and dark as charcoal, streaked low down with lurid yellow light and the trees on the Down threw up the white backs of their leaves in a lashing wind. Kay went by on his silver bike, among the drifting leaves. He still wore dark glasses but, ready for the oncoming rain, sported a transparent plastic mackintosh over his Levi suit which gave him the appearance of a very exotic and expensive orchid done up in cellophane. On his head he wore a large yellow souwester such as lifeboatmen wear to battle with the elements. He waved at Joseph. The heavens opened and the rain tipped down. Kay vanished.

'Come into that café over there,' she said.

'I haven't any money.'

'I'll buy you a tea only let's get out of this rain, for God's sake!'
She shook and shivered, hating the rain as much as a cat. You
could almost see her fur stand up. The sheeting rain spurted up
again from the roadway so it was difficult to see more than a few
yards and her light-grey jacket darkened with moisture on the
shoulders as he looked at her. Solly, impervious to the rain, got
up, yawned, stretched and made off to commit further mischief,
forgetting them.

They waited for a lull in the traffic and crossed over to the coffee shop, the first floor of which was a café, a soft, gentle,
half-tone place left over intact from the district's better days, full
of people one never saw anywhere else, as if they lived only
there and the waitresses stacked them neatly away on the shelves
with the willow pattern cups and saucers when the day was over
and the 'closed' sign went up on the door.

They mounted the Edwardian oak stair out of rain and dirt;
the warm, odorous inside of the shop was so completely another
world Joseph was appalled to see his doppel-ganger all at once
approaching him. There he was, walking towards himself; and
then he saw he and Anne were walking into their reflections in
a mirror he had forgotten existed in the café, a mirror in which
they made a pair of dream-like incongruity, a surreal wedding of
Loving Mad Tom and some primary school teacher he had
picked up who sang in the church choir in her spare time. Scum
from the standing pool tinged Joseph's black rags a ghastly green
but she looked more proper than ever, through she limped
dreadfully.

The tea-room, like the stair, was oak, with rush-seated, ladder
backed, William Morris chairs; willow pattern plates hung at
intervals upon the panelling and a beaten copper jug of
anemones (which Joseph knew from his book of facts were the
original lilies of the field which toiled not, neither did they spin)

stood on an oak dresser between plates of rock buns and sultana scones. A Yorkshire terrier yapped pettishly at Joseph from the cover of a tablecloth; then it stuck out its head and he saw a flat ribbon bow decorating its fringe so he kicked it mercilessly. He and Anne sat beside a window and watched the rain. When their tea arrived, she poured it out and filled the pot again from the hot water jug with pinched, stiff yet feminine gestures like a helper at a Whitsun treat or street coronation tea. This made Joseph feel like they had something, however tenuous, in common, a background of similar events.

'I hate the rain,' she said. 'Oh, how I hate the winter rain.'

She took off her jacket and hung it on the back of her chair to dry. Under her jacket she wore a short-sleeved blouse of ivory artificial silk fastened at the neck with a small pottery brooch in the shape of a pink rose. The old ladies chatted in subdued voices and shared rock buns warty with charred currants with their pet dogs. The grey day shone again from battered hotel silver surfaces of teapots and milkjugs. Joseph warmed his hands on his cup. He could not remember when he had last seen so many old ladies all together under one roof. Each chair seemed decorated with a propped walking stick.

'I hate the winter and love the sun,' she said stridently as if determined to have a conversation. Joseph marvelled how he had ever mistaken her surly self-sufficiency for shyness. What was she like on a sunny day? Did she bronze and glow?

'We get so little sun in England,' he said. 'It's a weepy kind of country.'

'That's a fancy way of putting it,' she said with disdain. 'I daresay it is just that we are in the rainy belt, geographically speaking.'

At that, as if cued in by this weather debate, Mrs Boulder entered the restaurant. Joseph had never seen her before outside the pub by the river or the living-room of her own flat, never before seen her by chance; in his mind, she always occupied her single cell in the honeycomb, always invariable, unmoving, like a statue or a tree, wrapped in this intangible cloak of loneliness or melancholy detachment. Now here she was in dazzling white on steel heels as high as a kite in this unlikely tea-room accompanied by a middle-aged man in a navy-blue suit. She processed in the stately manner of one about to launch a ship or open a fête. She looked straight through Joseph; she did not wish to acknowledge any of her son's beatnik friends today.

'She must be on the job,' said Joseph.

This seemed sufficiently extraordinary but he was very hazy about the details of her occupation and only knew she did a good deal of social entertaining, never less than a perfect lady. Or perhaps he was her accountant. Or her gynaecologist. Or something. She and her companion chose a secluded table and earnestly conversed. Joseph saw splashes of mud on her sheer stockings and the hem of her skirt. She shrugged off her white shiny mac.

'Do you want another cup?' asked Anne whose hands were veiny, freckled and old while Mrs Boulder's hands were smooth and white as pillows. He did not look like an accountant. Perhaps soon her Dunlopillo hands would be caressing beneath his Burton's suit the swine now buttering his crumpet with the air of a man of the world. Or maybe the deed was done already in his car on the Down while rain sluiced down the wind-screen and pattered on the roof. She eviscerated an eclair with a warped fork. Anne had forgotten him and gazed at rain and clouds with an expression of helpless spite on her face. There was the clear outline of a boat in the tea leaves on the bottom of Joseph's cup; a journey? Impossible.

'The sky is beginning to clear a bit, it's blowing over,' said Anne. 'We can go home.'

The word 'home' with its connotations of warmth and security came strangely fossilized out of her mouth of stone. 'I'm with her,' said Joseph to the aged waitress; she paid the bill impassively. As they left, Joseph could not help glancing once more at Mrs Boulder, who raised her head at that moment and met his eyes; he dived straight through these windows open on the virgin forests of her mind as if falling through a fantastic country of late medieval blues and greens, coming at last to rest upon a lawn beside a fountain where a young girl in a white dress trimmed with pearls cradled in her lap the horned head of the lascivious unicorn without knowing what he represented. This whole waking dream was compressed into the second in which their eyes communicated before she turned away her head. An ill-cemented curl began to tumble from her Martello tower of hair; maybe the whole painfully assembled fortification of sophistication was about to collapse entirely now she had revealed how fragile her defences were. She put her hand up to her hair; an expression of terror crossed her face.

'Come on!' said Anne, impatiently. The rain was over and the street glistened. She refused to take his arm again, saying she could manage alone, now, as the sit-down had done her good. She marched along lopsidedly like a wounded soldier off to fight in a forlorn hope.

'This is too much,' said Joseph, seeing Sunny. 'Hurry, get away before he sees us.'

But it was too late. Sunny waved his stick from over the road outside Marlene Coiffeuse. He was a walking accusation but he did not know it. The incident of the cigarettes must have been forgiven or forgotten; Sunny smiled and waved his stick. He had got his cap back or somebody had given him a new one exactly the same as the old. Rain dripped off the peak. Behind him, the wax head in Marlene's fly-blown window mimicked his beams. He looked like a child's drawing of an old man, a rectangle with arbitrary feet stuck on at one end and a blob at the other for a head. Fortunately, the flow of traffic prevented him crossing the road to speak to them.

'You've a funny lot of friends.'

'What's that?'

'Whores and tramps,' she said censoriously.

'Beggars can't be choosers, you know.'

'You're a little boy lost,' she stated categorically.

'But you hardly know me!' he remonstrated, hurt.

'I use my eyes.'

He recollected Gilchrist's *Life of Blake* and reprimanded her sharply: 'The eye sees more than the heart knows,' wondering if it were true; at any rate, it shut her up for she sniffed loudly but made no reply. They parted at the door of her room.

'Thank you for the tea, Anne,' said Joseph, obscurely glad to have a chance of using her first name. 'Look, I'll buy a drink some evening when I've got my money.'

It seemed exceedingly improbable to him she would accept this invitation and, in fact, she crisply snapped: 'T.T.' and banged the door.

From his window, he saw the rain-clouds scurrying back to the hills and the lifting mists revealed a play-time small and clean city. He lit his fire and his clothes began to steam. He felt very feverish and recalled that, in his childhood, hot baths were considered prophylactic against influenza; incoherently he decided to take a bath and wandered down to the communal bathroom. This was a tall narrow place, a slice off a room once a Regency drawing-room. There was a moulded frieze of cupids and ivy at the top of two walls. Peeling cream paint made crazy patterns on the walls. The monstrous geyser lit with a dithering crack. Joseph idled around the bathroom waiting for the bath to fill, examining the spongebags of the unknown other occupants of the house without curiosity, and was bored with the idea of bathing long before the water was ready but he noticed the cistern of the lavatory was embossed with the brand name or command, STANDFAST, so was forced to go through with it. He stripped off his sodden garments and immersed himself. The house in the late afternoon was unnaturally quiet. In the bath he felt insecure, remembering Marat's assassination, although he admired Charlotte Corday, and was disturbed to see the bathroom door pushed open; but it was only his cat.

She leapt up on the rim of the bath and sat neatly between the taps, above the soap dish, regarding him with such peculiar fixity Joseph became ill at ease and asked her not to look. She purred to hear his voice and tight-rope-walked around the rim of the bath towards him; she stepped less gracefully than usual and her flanks bulged. Were there more kittens already curled up, moist and tender, like baby ferns, inside her? He pictured the convoluted interior of her womb clotted with clutches of seed. She left five-fingered paw marks along the white enamel. She crouched beside his ear, purring raucously, and began to lick his shoulder with her little, rasping tongue. He stroked her soft front fur where the nipples stuck out.

'Are you affirming life again, in the pud again, snow white?'

He wondered if amniotic fluid was cosy as a good hot bath; perhaps more so. 'I'd like a house with hot and cold running amniotic fluid in all the bedrooms,' he thought. Propped against the side of the bath, he presently fell into a doze and dreamed he was back at the café with Anne or perhaps another girl he could not see clearly; perhaps it was Charlotte. Only, if so, he could not recognize her. They ordered ice-cream and, when the glass dish appeared, there lay Mrs Boulder in her vanilla-coloured suit. Her eyes were closed and her hands crossed upon her breast. As soon as he picked up the wafer biscuit, the bowl began to grow; soon it covered the table. He dug the spoon in about her navel. She was very rich and creamy to taste. The more he ate, the larger she grew.

The shadowy face of the other girl disappeared. Joseph realized he would have to clamber inside the bowl to continue eating as the bowl was now far bigger than the table and still growing in size. He did so. His heels squeaked, slithered and skidded. Cliffs of ice-cream now towered above him. His little spoon was woefully inadequate. He cast it aside and scooped up greedy fistfuls of Mrs Boulder's delicious viscera, cramming his mouth full, but suddenly he realized this creamy snow was melting; before he could escape a shuddering avalanche swept down upon his head, and he was gone for good, dead and buried all at once in the polar night of Mrs Boulder's belly.

He sank once more beneath the waterline, went right under the surface of the bath water (now grown cold) and woke in a flurry of wet. The cat leapt away from the waterdrops. When the convulsion cleared, he saw Anne standing beside the bath. It was almost dark. Her pale face and suit of pale grey flannel glimmered; she looked grim and ghostly. She thrust him a towel as if it were a dagger.

'There you go again,' she said. 'First you blow yourself up, then you drown yourself.'

'I'd have had to persevere, to drown in a domestic bath,' said Joseph angrily.

'They ought to pay me danger money, living with you.'

She clumped out of the bathroom and back up the stairs, every tensed muscle of her back suggesting offended disapproval.

Time passed, the weeks slid by as indistinguishable from each other as raindrops and, like raindrops on a windowpane, blurred together.

The cold spell set in bitterly; on the Friday morning, when Viv and Joseph stood together in the queue at the Labour Exchange, the air was like steel. Viv's ears, two crimson roses, sprouted from a Balaclava helmet of navy-blue wool. He had mittens to match. His mother had knitted them for him when he was perhaps twelve. He drew an apple from his pocket, polished it on the breast of his jacket (a cheerful mackinaw of red plaid) and offered Joseph a bite. The apple was extremely satin green, sharp and sweet. They crunched and shuffled forward.

'On the wall in this public lavatory, I saw written up: "I sucked off a dog, it was all right",' offered Viv in a conversational tone, determined to cheer Joseph up with a fact or two.

'It takes all sorts,' responded Joseph absently, looking at the apple, which began to swell until it resembled a green world. 'This reminds me of the hospital, I wish it hadn't. I don't want to remember the hospital any more. I saw a man in the hospital just this colour, his liver was screwed up, somehow. I'd never have thought it was possible for a man to turn this colour green. But he was sort of mottled, more like an avocado pear than this apple, really.'

Viv took back the poison apple with a sigh. Behind them, an old man began to cough his heart up, an endless, roaring, defiant, seismic upheaval at the conclusion of which he erupted a shimmering hillock of phlegm on Joseph's foot. Taken aback, Joseph snapped angrily over his shoulder: 'Better in than out.'

Then he saw the old man wore only pieces of separate suits, chalk-striped chocolate-brown jacket, Prince of Wales check trousers, cracked blue waistcoat without an overcoat against the cold and was already apologetically muffling a fresh cough in a less than clean handkerchief. When the old man recovered, he said: 'Sorry, son, it's the lungs, see. Poor old lungs gone as rotten as gorgonzola, I'm getting on, getting on, see.'

'That's all right, skip, don't apologize,' muttered Joseph, who felt his heart was being slowly squeezed in a press.

'It's the lungs,' continued the old man with a dreadful humility, preparing to hawk again.

'For God's sake, don't apologize!' howled Joseph. The old man, roused, dropped his handkerchief.

'Who do you think you fucking are?' he demanded aggressively. 'Think you're Lord Fucking Muck, taking that tone with me, a kid like you?'

'Oh, Christ, shut up, Joseph, give him a fag or something and don't say you're sorry!' whispered Viv, very ill at ease. The old man immediately squared up to Viv.

'And no cheek out of you,' he began but was temporarily paralysed by a renewed fit of coughing which reduced him to a trembling wreck and he had to lean against the wall. He had just a few strands of grey and white hair brushed neatly across the top of his skull. The queue inched forward and the sick old man was left behind.

'The trouble with you is your eyes fill too easily with compassion,' said Viv. 'What I think is, that you can only feel sorry for people you despise.'

Joseph had never heard him speak so bitterly. Viv flashed him a look of censure.

'I bet those lepers hated St Francis,' he added unexpectedly. 'Fancy having a perfect stranger come up and kiss you just 'cos you've got a skin infection, just to show off what a big heart he had, you never hear the leper's side of the story. What if a leper out of the blue had jumped up and kissed St Francis, I bet St Francis would have been ever so affronted. What a pig. Here, there goes Kay on his bike.'

Weaving an intrepid path in and out of the traffic, Kay sped by in the snug camouflage of his pea-green and khaki army

surplus paratrooper's jacket; a string bag bulging with groceries was strung across his handlebars and a great bunch of
holly was tied to the saddlebag. He nodded cheerfully to them
both. A few drops of freezing rain began to fall. A preposter-
ously fat man before them in the queue farted loudly and
malodorously. Then a rolling tramp broke line with a fierce
shout and pushed past them along the pavements, jostling and
frightening washed pedestrians; he caught hold of another a
few yards farther on by the frayed collar of his coat and shook
him.

'Where did you get to last night?' he asked in a broad Scots
accent. 'I say, where did you get to? I woke up on the Down and
it was three in the morning and everything freezing and the fire
gone out and Sid Walker gone. Watt gone, you gone, I was all
alone, poor Jock by himself, why did you go and leave me all
alone among the ashes?'

They tussled unsteadily and ineffectually for a minute or two
but soon stopped and stood together in deathly silence. The fat
man farted again, even more richly, shrouding Viv and Joseph in
a cloud of sulphur, but Joseph thought of the scene he had wit-
nessed on the Down the night he and Kay rescued the badger;
these two tramps in ragged coats were still, however vaguely, pro-
gressing in a straight line, still got their benefit, had still more
spiritual garments to shed before they reached that final state of
wooden nakedness.

'And Sunny is in fact a petit bourgeois, not a tramp at all,' he
said. 'He has a home and is quite smartly dressed. And there is
always the music to occupy him.'

A beatnik at the back of the queue wailed out some snatches
of blues on a harmonica. The rain congealed to sleet and spat-
tered them like porcupine quills. The Scottish tramp, Jock,
began to groan loudly, swaying to and fro. Viv clasped Joseph's

shoulder for Joseph had turned his face away and picked agitatedly at the plaster between the red bricks of the Labour Exchange wall.

'Bear up, my lover, not long to wait, now.'

'You never reach the end, there is always something worse; down and down but always a new worse thing.'

'Don't speak so loud, they'll hear you.'

'It makes us different from the animals,' said Joseph in a voice taut with strain. 'A limitless capacity for enduring suffering.' Darts of sleet struck his face; the queue shuffled forward. Viv had to drag Joseph along with the moving double file as Joseph was trying to cling on to the wall.

'You talk like a rotten book,' said Viv with sudden extraordinary bitterness. 'Listen, Joseph, I'm only a poor prostitute's son –' he paused and amended this, 'a rich prostitute's son and not an intellectual like you by any means but I play my piano, I get my rations and I get by and that's what we all do, we do our turns, whatever they are, then wham! the show is over, goodnight. Will you come on, we're nearly there.'

'I dreamed I ate your mother.'

'What's that? What did you say?'

They halted almost outside the glass door. Joseph had more or less recovered, although he was breathing heavily. He looked at Viv's succinct hazelnut-shaped head and dark, gentle features, seeing as if for the first time in their long friendship the perfect comic sadness of the other's face. It was a face resigned to mortality. Around them, the old and hopeless staggered beneath a cruel pelting of keen blades of sleet and over the burned fields of the ricebowl of Asia the bombs unfurled a keener sleet of mutilation and Viv was resigned to all these facts of mortality; all at once Joseph was consumed with the desire to outrage him, to precipitate him from his vanquished calm.

'Vivvy, do you love your mother?' he began with treacherous sweetness.

'Oh, yes,' said Viv sedately. 'I'm quite sure of that, thank you, best mum in the world, bless her.'

Joseph crept crabwise against his friend, and, prompted by his angel, said: 'What about fancying her?'

'You've gone too far, this time!' yelped Viv, but by now they had reached the door itself and were swallowed up and separated inside. During the processes of acquiring the week's money, Joseph slowly woke to a state of tension and alarm. His relations with Viv had reached some rapids, even a waterfall, some grand confusion of resentment and dependence to whose approaches his preoccupation with terror had blinded him. The habit of friendship was harder to break and more irrational than that of love; by what curious means had he become necessary to Viv, how did he appear inside the round theatre of Viv's skull? Did his fragmented actions appear whole and all-of-a-piece to Viv, like any other performance of life might appear? But, chasing after Viv down the street, obsessed with these questions, he found Viv had closed over again, presenting a simple, bright, impervious surface to him, old friends, all secrets hidden.

'Kay's throwing a big party on Christmas Eve,' he said. 'We're giving him some music, the Electric Opera, that is. Got all the lights working lovely. It should be a nice party. You come along Joseph, it would do you good. You don't see enough people, my star, don't chat and laugh enough.'

'When is Christmas Eve, then?'

'Why, next week; didn't you know? Honestly, don't you remember?'

Over their heads, above a departmental store, an enormous papier mâché Santa Claus drew parcels from a sack surrounded by cardboard reindeer.

'I can't go home,' said Joseph. 'I'm in no state to listen to the Queen's speech in peace, or the service of nine lessons and carols, either.'

'You do look a bit wild. Get mum to clip your hair a bit, I should. I mean, enough is enough.'

'And is it really almost Christmas, the season of goodwill to men, on earth peace?'

'Too right,' said Viv sadly.

Then a strange apparition flashed past them, darting down the road like a humming-bird, a tall, long-legged girl in startling gaudy clothes. Dayglo green stockings, purple and orange smock and, wrapped loosely around her, a blanket or poncho of various brilliant wools. Her hair was a flying cloud of streaky marmalade colour; obviously a heavy application of yellow dye had half grown out. The sleet seemed to part to let her through without getting wet and she was running and laughing as though the cold exhilarated her and the fact of December even seemed amusing. They both stared after her; she seemed to leave a haze of colours on the air.

'I know her,' said Viv. 'She's Barbie. She's American, she's staying at Kay's house, she turned up from nowhere with two straw suitcases full of glass beads and paper flowers. A bloke on Paddington station gave her Kay's address. In the automatic cafeteria.'

On the way home, Joseph bought a piece of coley for his cat; when he took the newspaper wrapping from the fish, he saw a photograph which distressed him very much. It showed an American soldier holding a child in his arms although the child itself appeared to have no arms left. The face of the child was so bloody you could not tell what sex it was but that of the soldier was broad, freckled and not very bright. When he was the age of the child he held, he would have been the image of the archetypal

American schoolboy with snub nose and gap teeth who grins from hoardings: 'Gee, mom, what a swell dessert', or goes fishing with his father on the covers of magazines. Now, at less than Joseph's age, betrayed into murder, he accused the camera with a horrid surprise, bearing his victim in his arms, child and man both lopped trunks of mutilated innocence.

Joseph found a drawing pin and pinned this picture on the wall between Marilyn Monroe and the monk who burned but he soon found the eyes of his unknown soldier were following him about the room so he took it down again and laid it on the table. Outside the sleet had turned to rain and washed down the windows. There was a moaning wind. The gas fire popped and flared. Nothing could be seen of the city at all. He tried to read Gilchrist's *Life of Blake* because he thought it would calm him but he could not concentrate on the printing for it kept resolving itself into the lines of the picture of the soldier and he despairingly acknowledged that only the mute vocabulary of symbolism remained to express his unspeakable disgust.

Joseph and his grotesque angel conceived a bizarre joke; they decided to send a piece of excrement to Lyndon Johnson. Accustomed as he was to handling shit, it was (once the shit had been produced) a simple matter to box and pack a fair-sized turd. He used an empty cardboard box which had once contained cornflakes, the sunshine breakfast and as much newspaper as he could find. He had to sacrifice his whole pile of Vietnam cuttings and also a scrap book of facts in order to pack it up securely. He also packed the picture of the soldier and the child. He printed the words EAT ME on a piece of paper torn off a tea packet and placed it upon the turd. He laughed in a demonic fashion as he went about his task. The air parcel rates for this package cost him half his National Assistance allowance but it seemed to him a small price to pay.

'I sent a Christmas gift to the White House,' he said to Ransome.

'What was that?'

'Shit.'

'I'm sorry, I didn't catch what you said.'

'Shit, repeated Joseph. Across the leatherette table top which was the colour of dried blood they transfixed each other's gaze, and Joseph perceived in the melancholy concern of Ransome's white eyes that if the psychiatrist were allowed to believe him, Joseph's actions would be translated from ironic moves in a black farce to ideas of real madness.

'It was such a vivid dream!' said Joseph with conviction. 'I almost smelled it and was so relieved, I can tell you, to wake up and smell only the usual one of graves around my pillow. The same night, I dreamed I ate my best friend's mother.'

'Did you enjoy her?' asked Ransome impassively.

'She was too much for me, she swallowed me up.'

'I'm neither a Freudian nor a shaman, I don't pretend to interpret dreams.'

Was the danger past? Ransome moved in his chair and his glasses caught the light, momentarily flashing like searchlights or headlights; he was a car travelling in the opposite direction. He passed by Joseph on the other side of the road. Charlotte had the same air in their last days together, she finally passed beyond contact. Unlike parallel lines, they would not even meet at infinity.

5

Joseph counted his money and found there was enough so he knocked on Miss Blossom's door; he knew she was at home by the leaks of light around the door frame but she did not open to him immediately. There was a rustling inside the room and the sound of drawers jamming as if clumsily closed in a hurry, concealing everything.

'Oh,' she said without surprise or pleasure. 'It's you.'

'Come down to the pub,' said Joseph as invitingly as he knew how. He had washed his hands and face.

'I told you. I don't drink.'

'Have a gin and orange,' he hazarded, since this was a favourite drink at office parties.

'Why are you pestering me?' Joseph could not see her face as the light was behind her and streamed around her; she seemed a very tall, black figure like a wooden schoolmistress or Mrs Noah from a nursery ark.

'Oh, come on, love,' he said, irritated. 'Give yourself a break.'

Amazingly she relented. 'All right,' she said and put on her coat, which was of brownish tweed, while Joseph stood on the draughty landing, wondering what to do next.

'I haven't taken a bird out in months,' he said.

'I trust I'm not your bird.'

'You're not very friendly, you know,' he complained.

'I don't trust friends,' she said. They went downstairs slowly, because of her limp.

'What do you think of the war in Vietnam?' he asked.

'I've got sorrows of my own.'

'But which side are you on?'

'Don't bother me with wars in foreign places,' she said petulantly. 'I lost a father in the last one. Or,' she added in a voice more hesitant than Joseph had ever heard from her, 'I may have lost a father, I mean, I, may have, I mean, it's possible and seems likely ...'

Her voice trailed into silence. In the dim light of the weak bulb in the hall, her face was open, soft and woundable; Joseph had not seen her look as if anything could hurt her before. Now, somehow, she had tricked herself into vulnerability.

'May I hold your arm?' she said. 'My leg doesn't half feel bad.'

When she heard footsteps in the hall, the admiral's daughter in the first-floor front twitched her blinds and looked out of the window to see who it could be. Joseph saw the movement of the curtains in the darkened room. The old lady could not afford to light her room in the evenings; she sat in front of a few red lumps of coal, revisiting Australia, New Zealand and Pacific islands where little brown naked boys dived for halfpennies off the dock.

'Today I caught the admiral's daughter feeding my cat on breast of chicken though she hasn't enough money to buy proper food for herself,' said Joseph. 'But she said my cat needed rich food because it's going to have some more kittens.'

'If she's so fond of cats, why don't you give her one, a kitten, when they're born.'

'She says a cat of her own would be a tie and stop her going on voyages.'

'But she never leaves the house.'

'I know. Would you like a kitten, Anne?'

'No,' she said firmly.

'It would be something to love,' tempted Joseph.

'No, never, thanks all the same,' she said sharply.

A boat on the river sounded its melancholy horn. The immense black sky was splintered with icy December stars; it was very cold. The twiggy thickets in the garden made a dry susurration like the rustling of old newspapers.

'Legend relates that Odin hung up on a tree for nine nights, strung between heaven and earth, and learned various secrets,' said Joseph.

'What's that got to do with me?' said Anne.

'Are you going home for Christmas?'

'I am an orphan and was brought up in Barnado's.'

'Oh. Oh. I'm sorry.'

'Accidents happen,' she snarled.

Stung by the unexpected ferocity of her tone, Joseph replied: 'I'm not sorry, in fact. I don't care at all, why should I. I don't give a toss.'

'You can't say plainer than that, can you,' she said, apparently mollified, for some reason. 'Are you going home yourself, better have a good wash before you go home.'

'Oh, my God,' he said. 'Don't bring me down.' There was still the letter to write. I am afraid I cannot make it home for Christmas this year but better luck next time, Mum and Dad ... I'm everso sorry, Mum and Dad, but circumstances prevent ... Bad news, Mum and Dad.

'They'd never understand,' he said. 'They'd think I did it on purpose to annoy them.'

'Do you love them?'

'I don't know. I don't see them much.'

'I only wondered,' said Anne. 'Not having a family oneself, see, one is always curious.'

'My friend Viv loves his mother,' said Joseph. 'But love is her business.'

'That's nothing to joke about!' she reprimanded so sharply Joseph was again reminded of a schoolmistress. He decided to glut her with family details and began in a sing-song chant:

'My father gets up so early in the morning it is still the night before and sorts the papers for the delivery boys. He marks each one with the address in a soft, black pencil. His hands are now permanently tinted a little bit grey with newsprint and he keeps a freshly sharpened pencil handy behind his ear all day, the point of which makes small black signs on his temple. In the shop, he wears a pair of carpet slippers bursting like bread at the joints of his feet.'

'Where are we going?' she interrupted.

'You're not listening to me at all,' said Joseph, in sorrow.

'Why should I?'

They walked down the hill, past terraces studded in lights. The tall rows of houses were like cliffs with fires of barbarians burning in the mouths of caves. Every single light was on in Kay's house as they went by and two girls stood outside in the cold air on the rickety balcony stringing up fairy lights. They laughed together in the light cascading from the uncurtained windows; it was the American girl, Barbie, and the small, fat girl, Rosie. Rosie wore jeans and a tee shirt, as usual, but Barbie had on a loose dress of brilliant green velvet which glowed like wet moss. They were playing Chuck Berry on a very loud gramophone inside the house. Then Barbie plugged in a socket and the fairy lights came on, electric strawberries, lemons, grapes, redcurrants, roses and magic lanterns winking and blinking at random.

'What a terrible din,' said Anne.

'They're going to give a big party.'

'Sounds as though they're having it now.'

'No, they're just getting ready.'

'There was always a Christmas tree six foot high at the Home,' said Anne. 'It was covered in lights just like those lights and tinsel and artificial snow. Underneath were all the presents kind people gave us, used toys and that. Then Santa used to come and reach each of us something out of his sack.'

'My grandfather used to pack a sock for me when I was very young. It always contained an orange, an apple, some almonds and brazil nuts in a twist of paper with holly on it, a rubber ball, a Superman annual, a potato gun, a bar of fruit and nut chocolate and a cracker sticking out of the top. It never varied. Who'd have thought I'd have the list by heart. Then he died, of course.'

'Did he live with you?'

'Until I was six.'

'It was a real family, then.'

'Everything complete. He was a very respectable old man. He had to have everything nice, clean shirts and so on. He drove my mother wild making her starch his shirt collars just so. He said he'd bequeath me the gold watch they gave him on the railways, for a retirement present but when they told him he had cancer, he broke the watch, dropped it on the concrete in the backyard and jumped on it. "Time's done no good to me," he said. Then he said he was going out to get drunk though usually he never touched a drop except Christmas and weddings. But my mother was crying so he stayed at home and watched the television quite peacefully with us.'

'Does that sad whore go to this pub?'

'Sorry?'

'That whore. The one in the café that time.'

'Oh, Mrs Boulder. Yes, she does, but she's usually busy at holiday times.'

'Well, I'm sort of curious because she might be my mother, too, see,' said Anne. Joseph realized with astonishment she was making a grim, sad, frosty joke. In the dark lane between the garden walls, they flushed old Sunny from a patch of deep shadow. He was resting.

'My poor old ticker,' he said. He moved slowly and painfully towards them. 'If you had my poor old ticker, you wouldn't walk so fast, you young people.'

'Are you still my friend?' asked Joseph.

'Now and then,' said Sunny. 'I know you, you used to go around with a blonde young lady.' He pursed his lips and gave a wolf whistle. 'A blonde young lady not like this one at all,' he said emphatically.

'This is Miss Blossom,' said Joseph. 'Miss Blossom, this is Sunny Bannister.' The introduction seemed bare; he added, to bulk it out: 'Sunny plays the violin.'

'Playing the fiddle is like courting a young lady,' said Sunny promptly, going into his old busking act at once. 'You got to love a fiddle. Stroke its belly gentle. Just like when you're new married, you have a bit of trouble with your bow, not stiff enough, your bow, but practice makes perfect. Eh? Then, after you've finished, you wipe off your bow with a rag.'

At the conclusion of this short monologue, he was wheezing with laughter in the starlit lane, nudging Joseph conspiratorially with his elbow, but when he saw Anne's stern face he hushed and mumbled: 'No offence, lady. No offence, mum. Mam.'

'I think you're perfectly disgusting,' she said.

'In my youth, I was the double of the Prince of Wales,' said Sunny aggressively. 'And a real lady-killer, I can tell you.'

'Summer's gone, dad,' she said. 'Winter's come.'

'It's never winter in my heart,' said Sunny. 'If you had a fiddle, I'd play you a tune.'

He wheezed with suspicious mirth again but Anne sneered: 'I bet you can't play a note.'

'Why am I wasting my time with this ill-tempered bitch?' thought Joseph.

Very slowly, they at last arrived at the public house. All the paper decorations were up; the public bar, into which Sunny led them, had an entire false ceiling of yellow, green, pink and lilac paper chains and garlands, looped up and around like hangings in the tent of Genghis Khan. Cut paper bells hung at intervals above the bar which was lavishly decorated with silver paper fringes, small glass balls and artificial holly, ivy and mistletoe. The radiators sent out a roasting heat and an electric fire, wedged in the grate, made two red fingers of warmth. The barman wore a sprig of mistletoe behind his ear; Joseph had not realized Christmas had begun. A large sign said: A JOLLY YULETIDE TO ALL OUR PATRONS; 'that's nondenominational,' said Joseph to Anne but she did not laugh or even smile. She asked for grapefruit juice. Sunny had a half of cider. He looked like a glum child.

'I played in many leading orchestras before crowned heads,' he said. 'The Queen's Head. The King's Head.'

'Street busking and pubs,' sneered Anne. 'I knew it.' She broke unexpectedly into cheerless song.

> *Put another nickel in*
> *In the old man's treacle tin,*
> *When he plays his violin*
> *It's murder, murder, murder.*

Rachel face powder was clogged in pink grains on her upper lip and lipstick had smudged on to her teeth. She took dainty precise sips of juice.

'I don't know any other girls who wear lipstick,' he said. She was only twenty-three or -four, all the time. 'Not girls as young as you, that is. Mrs Boulder covers herself with it.'

'I always say lipstick finishes you off,' she said.

'Quids, we used to make,' said Sunny. 'Quids and quids, pass round the hat, in come the money. Chink, chink.'

He was clearly delighted to have a captive audience. He began to play his imaginary fiddle and, at the same time, he sang 'Waiting for the Robert E. Lee'.

'There's daddy and mammy and Ephraim and Sammy ...'

'Do you want another half, you silly old man,' said Anne brusquely.

'Thanks, ducks. You old cow,' he added under his breath. He went on playing. Anne bought the drinks; the bar was beginning to fill with revellers and they retreated to a table beside the juke-box.

'At the Home, we used to sing, "On Top of Old Smokey",' said Anne and, to drown Sunny, began to sing:

> *'On top of old Smokey*
> *Where nobody goes,*
> *I saw Betty Grable*
> *Without any clothes.'*

Sunny lowered his fiddle.

'You filthy beast,' he said. 'Now I'll play you a waltz. It's my favourite waltz, a lovely waltz, it's called "Sweet Dreamland Faces". I wrote up to Harry Davidson to play it on the wireless but he didn't, bet he didn't know it.'

He hummed the tune as he played which was just as well since otherwise they would never have heard it.

'I'll tell you a joke,' said Anne to Joseph over Sunny's head. 'I was the cleanest baby you ever saw in the cleanest carrier bag and I lay on Barnado's step and pinned on my very clean shawl was this note that said, "Please take good care of my little blossom". So they gave me Blossom for my surname, see.'

'How savage you are,' said Joseph in wry admiration. She seemed more mysterious than ever, an articulated doll of flesh and bile.

'Lovely young waltz,' panted Sunny in conclusion.

'Oh, shut up,' she said. 'Shut up or buzz off.'

'I saw you in the garden, once,' said Joseph. 'Early in the morning.'

'I am a nature lover,' she said austerely. 'That is why I am so fond of the Down.'

'Now I'll sing you a comic song entitled "Far, far away",' said Sunny desperately, seeing their attention wandering away from him. He immediately began to sing:

'Where is my mother-in-law?

– now I want you all to join in, all to join in with –

Far, far away!
Where is her nagging jaw?

– come on, now, have a bit of fun, all join in –'

'Look, I told you to buzz off so buzz off before I complain about you to the publican and have you slung out.'

A look of infinite cunning crossed Sunny's face.

'Give us a kiss,' he said.

'All right,' said Anne, abruptly smiling. She allowed him to kiss her forehead, which seemed to restore all his good humour.

'Now go away,' she requested; he stumbled to his feet.

'Night night, beautiful,' he said. 'Nighty night, young man.' He moved off slowly into the crowd, which was now dense and talkative.

'Whew,' she said. 'Thank God he's gone. He ought to stay at home and not come out depressing people.'

She gloomily drank her juice. Joseph, too, began to feel low. Sunny's bad performance of entertainment, memories of childhood and the oppressive noise and laughter around them combined to make him feel intolerably sepia-coloured and two-dimensional. He felt his consciousness might very well soon slip its moorings and drift off from his body like an errant balloon; it was a breathless feeling. He touched the cool sides of his glass with a stranger's fingers and saw the worn pile of his coat as if it were somebody else's coat altogether and the arm in it that of another man.

'Help me,' he said violently to Anne. 'Make me feel real, somehow.'

'What do you mean?' she said. 'What a line! What a pass!'

There was a sudden bustle at the entrance and a band of Irish came in, wearing best navy-blue suits; a girl with them was playing a flimsy small tune on a tin whistle. Across her back was slung a red enamelled melodeon. The men surged to the bar; the girl put away the tin whistle, unslung her melodeon and began to finger out music from it. Joseph heard the Irishmen calling her Maggie.

She wore a pale-blue woollen cardigan thin at the elbows and frayed at the cuffs over a pale-blue dress with shiny threads in it. Flat flowers made of the same material as the dress decorated the baby collar. It must have been a very cheap dress for it was badly creased and wrinkled, and it was far too long, cutting into her bulky legs at the thickest part; when she was a little older, her legs would be pulpy, heavily veined and discoloured, and she wore shiny, sheer, unflattering stockings with a run in the left leg. Her shoes were heavy black leather, ungainly and keeling over at the heels. She wore big, dangly ear-rings like Christmas tree decorations and her hair was a fountain of amber, arching from a high, round forehead, a Stuart forehead like those of women in Lely portraits and she had the same colouring, a milky skin and pale-blue, rather prominent eyes, which the dress must have been chosen to match. It was a tilted, brazen face, a carefree slut's face; she was a raw-boned country girl, very young and very rackety, the spirit of Saturday night in small country towns at the back of beyond, a neighbourhood bad girl meaning no harm. Perversely, she seemed like Anne to Joseph, as though Anne, happy, could have been like this. Maggie wandered among the merrymakers picking out music they could not hear because of the noise from the juke box.

'I will have a gin this time,' Anne said. 'Perhaps strong drink will cheer me up.'

Joseph looked at the girl in blue and remembered a picture he had once seen of a bird with blue plumage called Prince Rudolph's blue bird of paradise. Mechanically he went to the bar for Anne; when he got back to the table, Maggie was leaning against the juke box. Her face was flushed; she smiled at Anne out of a surplus of happiness and they looked like sisters, the fast one and the disapproving one. There was a gap between records; Maggie began to play and sing. She had a strident voice like honey on the blade of a knife. She was loving to show off and shone with exuberance. All the Irishmen joined in her song. She vamped out a thumping waltz time on the bass and sang with a brisk, pure lack of sentiment:

> *He went upstairs to go to bed*
> *And found her hanging from a beam,*

> He took a knife and cut her down
> And in her bodice a note he found.
>
> 'I wish I wish but it's all in vain,
> I wish I was a maid again;
> But a maid again I'll never be
> Till cherries grow on an apple tree.
>
> 'Dig me a grave both wide and deep,
> A marble stone at my head and feet
> And in the middle a turtle dove
> To tell the world I died of love.'

The Irishmen cheered. Joseph looked at Anne and saw fat tears descending her cheeks. She took the drink and dumbly shoved it to the girl, Maggie, who accepted it as her due and drank it down.

'Take me home,' Anne said. She was an ugly weeper; the tears came reluctantly and her face screwed up in piteous, Gothic folds like weepers in medieval carvings and also became blotched and scarlet. She was trying to make as few sounds as she could. They left at once. Outside a fierce wind was blasting the river road and there was nobody in the street. The lights were out in the Boulders' flat above the used car saleroom. Anne scrabbled for her handkerchief; when they reached the secrecy of the lane, she gave way wholly to tears, choking and wailing, pressing fists into her eyes and rolling her head from side to side. She leaned against the wall and tears splashed on to the ground. When Joseph touched her, she pushed him away with all her might. She cried as hard as she could for five minutes; then she subsided, hiccoughing, and scrubbed her face with her handkerchief.

She leaned on Joseph but more for support than comfort;

they walked up the lane past Kay's house which was now, for some reason, in complete silence and darkness, except where the fairy lights glimmered. Their footfalls made small sounds which, as they walked on without exchanging a word, seemed to Joseph more and more perfidious until finally he identified the menace as distant gunfire, again. Desultory gunfire, sniping. The hallucination took hold of him with such force it seemed that every step he took sent a lazy bullet whining from a rifle. At no special target, at nothing but a few ripples of movement, leaves moving in the sweet Oriental wind scented like jasmine tea mixed with blood. And sometimes there would be an answering crack of a bullet and sometimes a scream and sometimes only the leaves still flowing as if nothing had happened. Step by step, the bullets sprayed. A cry. Or was it the wind? Or a cry?

'Stop,' he said. 'I can't go on.' He saw her plain face ravaged by tears; he was almost out of his mind. 'I know you've lost a child,' he said.

'I didn't lose it,' she answered. 'I gave him away. My son. Tell us the old, old story. It's too cold to stand still, Joseph, it is so cold it makes my head ache. We must go home.'

Now she was the stronger. Her hand was a clue leading him through a labyrinth; they bypassed a rain of shot and arrived at their house.

'Come into my room,' she said. 'You look awful.'

He lay on her bed face down.

'Mind your filthy shoes on my quilt,' she chided. 'I bet you never clean your shoes. I'll make a nice cup of tea.'

When she returned from the kitchen, with the teapot and cups, he was deeply pressed into the lumpy bed as if trying to sink into the actual substance of the mattress and disappear altogether from sight. She put her tray down on the dressing-table and sat on the bed beside him. She laid her hand on his shoulder; he flinched convulsively.

'Joseph,' she said, very gently, for her. 'What is the matter with you?'

'I don't know,' he said in a muffled voice.

'Well, it's quite safe to come out,' she said with a touch of irony. She got up and poured herself some tea. After a while, Joseph rolled on to his back and watched apprehensively the stains on the ceiling.

'My girl walked out on me when I needed her most,' he began, trying out a new theory.

'When was that?'

'When she was pregnant. Can I have some tea?' He thought: 'That is what might have happened, though it never did.'

'Was it your kid?'

'She said I'd make a lousy father. She got a first.'

'Pardon?'

'In her examinations. We were both students. She took being a student very seriously but, all the same, it was pretty vulgar of her to do so well.'

'Are you telling the truth?' she asked suspiciously, stirring his tea with those skimped, tight gestures.

'Anyway, she left me,' said Joseph defiantly. 'Then I worked in the hospital cleaning up shit and amputations.'

'What happened to this baby?'

'What baby?'

'Your baby.'

He gave her the furtive look he usually reserved for Ransome.

'It was such a vivid dream,' he said, in the same voice of utter conviction.

'You're only a kid yourself,' she said.

'Don't give me that,' he said. He did not know how to explain his constant sense of guilt at being alive. Her gas fire breathed asthmatically. She took up her plastic bunny box; she did not know he had seen inside it. She recited:

> *'The Queen of Northumberland*
> *Gave the King of Cumberland*
> *A bottomless tin*
> *To put flesh and blood in.*

'Do you know the answer to that, Joseph?'

'No.'

'It's a ring,' she said. She took the gimcrack ring from the bunny rabbit box and slipped it on her finger. She waved her hand until the tiny diamond caught the light.

'My bloke deluded me with a ring and some promises that came even cheaper,' she said. 'As soon as he'd knocked me up, he beat it and left no forwarding address. There was no one in the world for me to turn to but the National Council for the Care of the Unmarried Mother and her Child.'

'Anne,' said Joseph, cut to the heart. 'Poor Anne.'

'I tell you no lies,' she said. 'Then they gave my little boy away to some woman that couldn't have kiddies of her own and all I have left is a lock of hair I made them give me. And it's only first hair, see, so it's not true; I mean, all this'll fall out and he'll grow another lot and it might not even be the same colour so it's not really his hair at all.'

'Anne ...'

'Sometimes the tips of my, you know, breasts hurt, they're sore; then I know he's crying. It's a sure sign, or so they say.'

'When did this happen to you? When was he born?'

'Three months ago. Then I came to a new town to start a new life, see. He'd be three months and three weeks old. I didn't want to keep him, mind; however could I keep him on the money I earn, in furnished rooms, sleep him in a drawer?

She thrust her hands inside the sleeves of her beige cardigan and hugged herself. Her face was peculiarly sharp and pinched. Joseph recalled photographs of the embryo in the womb, the first regard from an eye without eyelids, the fleecy lanugo down, such small beginnings. It seemed an act of savage love to grow a child in the privacy of one's flesh for nine months, through three seasons of a year, and then to tear it out and give it away.

'What upset me most was not having to give up my little boy, nor bearing him, nor being deserted, nor being shamed, but being lied to and sponged off all that time. I thought I'd found somebody who cared about me but it was all lies and self-deceit. And now I'm a cripple, too, which I wasn't before, though I suppose I was never anybody's dream girl or pin-up, like.'

'How did you hurt your leg?'

'I fell down,' she said impassively: 'I fell down a flight of stairs, not that it did any good. It just crippled me. Did you read in the papers about that French girl who was in the family way so she jumped off the Eiffel Tower and all the doctors battled for weeks to save her life and the life of her child? Doesn't it make you sick? Only Catholics could be that cruel to a woman. They'd look at her and think of Eve and say, "It serves you right, you bitch, you've got to pay the price". Every time I looked at my baby's face, when I was in the Home, I thought of that smiling liar and could have died of anger. But all the same, my breasts hurt when the baby cries. At least, that's what I've heard. Like they can hear him crying for them.'

Joseph got up and poured more tea though by now it was cold and sour.

'Viv, my friend, is illegitimate. They get along, he and his mother. But then, she makes a lot of money.'

'Tits like hers are a licence to print it,' said Anne with contempt. 'I am a respectable girl.'

Suddenly she began to cry again.

'You know that rotten Pyrex ware with the rotten yellow roses? I bought it for my bottom drawer. I'd never had a kitchen of my own, see, always in rooms. He offered me a home.'

Joseph knelt beside her.

'Would you like me to stay here with you?' he asked. It took a huge effort to say this promising as it did the involvement of a kind he had altogether abandoned. Besides, he did not at all desire her, except that she was so unfortunate. She was so annoyed she stopped crying.

'No thanks!' she said roughly. 'That's the last thing I want!'

Joseph shrugged, not very much hurt.

'Well, can I do anything at all for you?'

'Get us a handkerchief from the top drawer,' she said, sniffing. She blew her nose loudly.

'All my actions are misconstrued,' said Joseph, looking out of the window at the boring top of the supermarket.

'I think you try too hard.'

'When I was a kid, I remember getting hold of this comic, the kind I wasn't supposed to read, the kind of comic American servicemen read for masturbatory purposes, I suppose. There was a story called "The Horror Dimension" where every nightmare you ever had came true, even the small ones, like halitosis.'

Anne took off her sensible shoes and groped beneath the bed with stocking feet for her blue felt slippers edged with imitation fur.

'It's good to get your shoes off at the end of the day. There are always the small pleasures.'

Joseph wandered around the miserable room until he came to the picture of Highland cattle. The far hills were blue with mist and red with bracken; in this eternal Highland autumn, no shots were fired or forsaken mothers wept; it was a very bad painting, one of the worst he had ever seen. He buried his head in his hands, making some muffled, yelping sounds but Anne said pigheadedly: 'I guess it's the small pleasures that keep you going, in the end,' and yawned. He was sharply furious with her.

'Look at my hands, look; they washed corpses.'

'I see your fingernails are still in mourning,' she said peremptorily. 'What's that to me? Death is perfectly natural.'

'How can you be so acquiescent?' he said angrily. 'After what you told me.'

'Don't go on so,' she said. 'I've had about a basinful of you tonight, Joseph. Here, I'll tell you another thing. If I thought my own natural mother was half as rich and beautiful as that tarty friend of yours, I'd be perfectly happy. I used to have all these fantasies in the Home about my parents while I was growing up, how my mother was a duchess or a countess or a famous film star and how she fell in love with someone beneath her, a soldier. A soldier who was killed in the war. And she couldn't support me so she gave away her little blossom. I dreamed I was a love-child, conceived in a sort of heart-shaped glow, and it didn't half keep me going, even after I grew up and realized it was a load of cock. So sometimes I think how my little boy will dream me into something lovely, something I never was.'

'Jesus wept,' said Joseph tiredly.

'Now I want to get my beauty sleep,' she said. 'Some of us have to work tomorrow, you know.'

'I certainly have the advantage of you there,' said Joseph. He lingered at the doorway, convinced there was a way of getting through to her. 'I suppose I could take you to this big party. Would you like that?'

'I daresay it would pass the time,' said Anne. She began to wind her hair round curlers.

6

Christmas Eve was so cold expelled breath hung in smoke signals on the frozen air. All the occupants of Joseph's house had abandoned it for the holiday except for Joseph himself, Anne and the admiral's daughter, who waylaid him to tell him of a Christmas in Mexico when her father was alive, with fireworks and processions, and he smiled and watched the ghosts of undernourishment undermining her face. He bought food from the pet shop to last his cat over the holidays and was depressed to see an emblematic sight there, a white mouse whizzing round in the trap of a treadmill. All the shops were crowded; Joseph bought bread and eggs and, on an impulse, six strange white foreign flowers with waxen petals and no perfume which he saw in a shop and wanted to give to Mrs Boulder. Then he had no money left at all and, when he rang his parents from a call box, had to reverse the charges.

There was a terrible few minutes incoherent back and forth between himself and his mother; when she realized he was telling her he would not be home, she began to sob, 'How can you do this to me, I've lost my boy.' He put the receiver down in bewildered embarrassment. He had not realized she would care so much. His mother was smallish and plumpish with greyish hair. She was a housewife and cleaned and cooked. When you fell over, you ran to her for Elastoplast, only she must have been younger, then, though it seemed to Joseph she must always have been exactly the same age and shape; and once he must have loved her more than anything in the world, had even lived inside her for nine whole months. This seemed most mysterious and unlikely.

At home, the shop would whisper with paperchains each time the door opened to let in a customer, last-minute purchases of cards and large Christmas boxes of chocolates, and his mother would be crying in the back room. In this room was a plaster donkey with plastic panniers containing everlasting flowers and also a Spanish costume doll in a mantilla and high comb, brought back from a fortnight on the Costa Brava. There was a different pattern paper on each of the walls, where the plaster ducks froze in flight. His mother would be sitting in front of the electric living-coal fire next to the hollow Dutch girl fire-stand and crying bitterly, as Anne cried. He had lived for eighteen years between the shop and the square of garden and, it seemed to him, had scarcely left a mark on the house to show he had been there, not a fingerprint on any wallpaper or a stain on the linoleum. Nothing. Only his mother crying because he was not there proved he had been there and gone. He fought with the impulse to ring her again to make sure. Only maybe his father would reply and at first repeat: 'We've always tried to do the best for you, son, always the best of everything', but would later break into a new formula, 'I'm going to wash my hands of you, Joseph, straight, I am.' So he did not ring up again.

Instead, he took the flowers to Mrs Boulder. There was a small brass knocker on her front door showing a piksy crouching on a toadstool with the word POLPERRO underneath it. She took a long time to answer the door and he smelled the whisky at once. It was well past the middle of the day but she was still clumsily bundled into a fantastic negligee straight from an erotic fantasy, a weird garment of salmon-coloured lace and prune-coloured satin. Her hair was down. Joseph had never seen her hair down before. It was quite long and stuck out about her shoulders in a stiff cloud. Repeated bleachings had given it a friable, tissue-paper or candy-floss quality, not like real hair at all but like the hair of a walking, talking doll. Last night's make-up was still on her face but blurred and askew with sleeping and, Joseph saw, weeping. Apparently every woman in the world was crying today.

'Viv's out,' she said. She examined the chipped ruby lacquer on her nails.

'I brought you some flowers,' he said.

'Gawd,' she said as if in wonder. 'You never.' He put the white parcel into her arms; she hugged it childishly, nervously, wondering what to do with so unexpected a present.

'Spending your money on me,' she said with ghostly reproof. 'But all the same, Joseph, it is everso nice of you to bring me flowers.' She was moist with tears as if every pore had wept.

'I don't know their names,' said Joseph. 'The girl in the shop told me but it was foreign and complicated and I've forgotten it. They're very white, anyway.'

There was some confusion of response between them. Their words seemed to fly away and dissolve like bubbles. They were both very nervous, never having been alone together before.

'Come in and have a drink,' she said as if reaching a decision in her mind. 'I'm celebrating.'

'Okay,' said Joseph.

'It's my birthday,' she said. Then, bravely: 'I'm forty-five.'

'No!' exclaimed Joseph for she looked perhaps five or six years older than this age or at least a well-preserved forty-five already. But she misunderstood him and thought he was surprised she was so old and at last consented to smile.

They went into the tiny kitchenette. The fold-down table in the breakfast nook was unfolded and covered with dirty dishes. Amongst the dishes was a bottle of Teacher's Highland Cream, half empty, and a small glass curded with lipstick. She took the white flowers and shook them from their paper; suddenly they looked like immortelles. She put them in the washing-up bowl and turned the tap on briefly.

'They must have a drink,' she said. 'So must we.'

She took another glass from a built-in cupboard. The kitchenette faced on to the docks road and had a dark outlook. Traffic thundered by all the time. Joseph's glass had a picture on it of a red-haired girl in a blue one-piece bathing-costume raising her arms above her head to dive off a high diving board. Mrs Boulder's glass, another of the same set, showed the same girl holding a red and white beach ball.

'There is a jug to match,' said Mrs Boulder, seeing Joseph curiously inspecting the glasses. 'Only I was never sure what to use it for so it never gets used.'

'At home, our glasses each have a different kind of flower and an ear of wheat on them. I bet these glasses came from the Co-op, like ours did.'

'However did you guess,' said Mrs Boulder absently. The angel of death appeared to her over the broken refrigerator; she tried to outstare him. Water dripped on to the floor out of the refrigerator door, which hung drunkenly on one hinge.

Lost in reverie, Joseph went on: 'We also have a large jug to complete the set and on it is a bunch of mixed flowers and several ears of wheat. When I was a kid, this was filled with lemon squash and ice-cubes at Sunday lunch. Or orange squash. At that time, ice-cubes were quite a big deal, in my part of South London, at any rate.'

She poured more whisky into his glass.

'But our glasses were of a kind of cut glass, not like these smooth ones, so as you drank from them you could see the world in dozens of warped facets.'

'I thought of slashing my wrists but then I thought not,' she said. 'Besides, I don't know whether it is a vein or an artery you are supposed to cut. And there was no hot water for a bath, anyway. You are supposed to do it in the bath, aren't you.'

'Why should you do this?' He thought: 'Nothing is sure, nothing.'

'I'm so afraid of growing old, Joseph,' she said simply. 'It starts when you are twenty-five or so and these first little lines come and you kid yourself for a few years they are giving you more character and you look sexier and more mature. But you have to touch up the grey hairs all the time. And then your neck starts to wither and sag. And your skin loses that lovely bloom, that freshness and bloom, and you have to use more and more make-up. It is like repairing a sandcastle. I am a sandcastle and the tide is coming in and obliterating me.'

'Look at me,' said Joseph. He was trembling with pity and nerves and an inexplicable fear; the room was full of her bad angels, grey beasts with pondwater eyes. Across the dirty dishes, they stared into each other's eyes again.

'I can see into your mind, where the dreams are,' she said in her dark-blue voice.

'I have bad dreams, terrible dreams,' said Joseph. They were both speaking very softly.

'Oh, yes,' she said. 'I know. You're the hanging man in the Tarot pack, you know what I mean?'

Joseph extended his hands to her, palms uppermost, inviting her to tell his fortune.

'It's all lies,' she said, taking his hands and running her fingers over the marks of the fire. As if absentmindedly, she continued to caress his hands as she spoke. 'The hanging man, ooh, he's a rotten card. He signifies destruction and ruins. He's bound by fate, he can't get free.'

Suddenly she flung her head back, defying unseeable demons.

'Screw me,' she said. 'Darling.' She began to cover his hands with burning kisses, pressing them to her face and breasts.

'Yes,' said Joseph for there was nothing else to say. The traffic roared by; the dishes danced with vibrations. She went on murmuring 'darling, darling,' in a choked babble, kissing his hands again and again. He had never been so afraid of dying. She sagged forward over the table, strands of her hair trailing in the bacon grease and tea dregs.

'I'm drunk,' she said. 'Oh, I don't know what I'm doing.'

'Don't tell lies,' said Joseph so brutally it brought her round and she took some deep breaths, glancing about suspiciously. Then they got up and went into her bedroom, which was cold as the tomb.

The wide bed was unmade, sour and rumpled. This room at the back of the house had a wide watery view of river, boats and warehouses. She went at once and pulled the curtains close, shutting out the light so they were in a black pod which contained them absolutely. But Joseph could hear intermittent choruses of gulls riding the currents of the heavens. This room was kinder than the kitchen. She switched on the electric fire; she knelt down on a goatskin rug watching the two red bars come to life. He knew she wanted this artificial night so he would not see the signs of age. The desperate boldness with which she had challenged him vanished; she seemed gentle and now either indifferent or sadly resigned to what she had provoked.

'I'm sorry it's so cold in here,' she said. 'But then, it's cold everywhere, today. Do you think we shall have snow? Do you think we shall have a White Christmas?'

Joseph was charmed she wished to protect herself with a little weather conversation. He approached her from behind and put his arms round her soft, extensive body, the breasts like shifting tumuli, the slack, slipping belly; she sighed.

'Take your things off, darling,' she said. 'Be naked for me because you're young and strong and thin and beautiful, my God, and young.'

He badly wanted to please her and exorcise her devils and give her some pleasure, like a being in her best dreams; he took off his clothes and knelt beside her for she herself showed no sign of moving.

'What is the trouble, love? What is it?'

Her eyes gleamed in the firelight, she was crying again.

'Oh, Jesus,' she said. 'I'm old enough to be your mother.'

'I'm sorry but let's worry about that afterwards, shall we,' said Joseph, losing his patience. He pushed her, yielding as foam, backwards on the rug and entered her then and there, in the intense cold; it was a fiasco. The fire sent out as yet no heat, only a dim, ruddy glow which covered them like blood and, in this uncanny illumination, the extraordinary tensions around them and the fantasy unlikelihood of it all subdued him. He came immediately and even felt a certain sardonic glee; in the duel of their angels, his shambling comedian had scored another triumph of black honour. But Mrs Boulder lay in a pool of lace, huge, white and wounded as a shot swan, and turned her head away.

'You're no bloody use at all,' she said. Her voice was rusty. 'I thought it would be all right with you as you're so young but you're no good, are you. The hanging man, ooh, he's a rotten card.'

'It was too much,' he said. 'I've not made it since Charlotte left, remember.'

'Huh,' she said.

'Let me try again in a minute, it'll be better, I promise you.'

'Promises are piecrusts, made to be broken,' she said. She hunched up in her negligee and darted beams of angry misery at him. Somehow they failed to touch him; now menace was gone. He did not know why, only sensed it, perhaps because disappointment made her behave rationally. She was not a hieratic figure in a frieze nor under demonic possession any more, she was simply disappointed. She was a fat, white, naked, middle-aged woman, now sober and, he realized, she had not defeated him and then he knew there was no reason why he should obey the Tarot pack. He took a cigarette from her without asking her and lit it from the fire. Curiously he touched the curdled skin of the vaccination mark on her right shoulder.

'Leave me alone,' she said, shrugging away from his hand but there was a backlog of too much affection between them; she sighed.

'Get into bed and get warm, I'll bring your drink.'

She tried to glare.

'Don't you order me about, Joseph Harker, I'm old enough –' she stopped short.

'Go on.' Joseph went to the door. She snorted and threw his shirt after him.

'Put something on,' she said. 'What do you think I am? I'm not having you running around in the altogether in my house.'

This seemed very funny to Joseph; he was still laughing as he took the white flowers from the sink and stuck each one in water in the girly glasses. He arranged these around the kitchen.

Then he piled all the dirty dishes in the sink, wiped down the table top and folded it back. He washed in the cold water and whistled a tune, Kay's tune, 'Pedro the Fisherman', why was that? He returned to the bedroom with her glass.

'I've not seen you look so cheerful for months,' she said disbelievingly. Hope, cold or despair had driven her under the blankets; the seagulls called and a boat hooted and he could see nothing of the room at all but the fur rug before the fire and big, vague shapes of bed, wardrobe and dressing-table with its shadowy gleam of mirror.

'Why were you sick over Charlotte that time, do you remember?'

'She used to look at me as if I had a heart of gold,' said Mrs Boulder. 'I thought, "I'll show her".'

'The day she left, she said to me: "I'm going to find a man who'll sit by the fire and say, 'Coom and give us kiss, luv,' now and then." But the last I heard of her, she was shacked up with some Polish Jew.'

'That's the same kind of thing, though,' said Mrs Boulder with wintry acumen.

'Yes; she was continuing her search for real people. She thought your obvious refinement was out of character, Mrs Boulder. I was rotten to Charlotte, I squandered all her allowance on pot and comic books and made fun of F. R. Leavis.'

'You preyed on her, you know,' said Mrs Boulder.

'Did I?' said Joseph, surprised.

'All she wanted was a bit of love, I expect, I mean, she was young.'

'Well, she came to the wrong shop, didn't she.'

'It was awful to see you together, she took everything so seriously and you were a right little beatnik, making fun of her all the time.'

'It didn't seem like that. Sometimes it seemed that all that mattered in the world was the space between her eyebrows, which was very clear, I can't explain, or the sunshine on the down on her forearms. At other times, these things were kind of memento mori, reminders everyone was slowly dying everywhere.'

'Christ, you were ever such a funny kid when my Vivvy first brought you round. The clothes you wore, you were a real scarecrow dandy, and she was so clean and pretty and you just used her as a punch bag, trying to get rid of the chip on your shoulder, I suppose.'

Joseph tried to recall Charlotte's face but it was no good, she was a blank in space. Not even a vampire any more; he no longer dreamed her making fat meals off his heart. And had it, in fact, been the other way around?

'You must have been watching us pretty closely, love.'

'After all, you were my Vivvy's friend,' she said. 'Of course I never liked her at all. She was everso affected.'

'It's funny, I've hardly thought of her for weeks and then I caught myself telling an elaborate lie about her to somebody last night, to try and explain. Or possibly to gain sympathy, I don't know. Yet I can't even remember her surname off-hand, it wasn't Corday. Did she have fair hair?'

'What were you trying to explain?' said Mrs Boulder.

Joseph, irritated beyond belief by this question, screamed: 'Shit!' Outraged, Mrs Boulder threw her glass at him, showering whisky everywhere; he saw it coming and caught it in his hand, like a conjuring trick. He looked at the glass and began to laugh again.

'By the way, do you want a kitten?'

'Oh, Joseph, you are terrible; when are you going to have that poor little thing doctored. It's not fair, forcing it to go on having kittens. Oh, my God, fancy. Poor little thing.'

'It's great to hear her purr when they all lie down and suckle.'

'Then you take her babies away.'

'Not till they're weaned,' he said gently.

'You're cruel,' she said.

'Maybe,' he acknowledged. It was a new idea to examine at his leisure.

Then there was a period of extremely deep silence in which even the faint hum of the electric fire and the distant tune from a transistor radio far away could be heard and seemed not to lessen but to intensify the silence until it began to exert a pressure like deep water on them both. This pressure grew and grew, hurting their eardrums, until Mrs Boulder cried out: 'No!'

Joseph rose from the rug and moved towards the bed.

'No,' she said. 'It's wrong, I'm a wicked woman leading you astray. No wonder it's no good with you, when it's so wicked. Go home, Joseph, go home, now.'

'I used to be very fond of Edgar Allan Poe,' said Joseph, 'I thought he knew the score. "Over the mountains of the moon, through the valley of the shadow, ride, boldly ride."'

He slid into the bed beside her; she squirmed away. The sheets were sticky, slippery nylon like a plastic bag and she could not move far enough to escape him so all at once clasped hold of him with most contemptuous energy, as though to get it over with quickly but Joseph knew, this time, he was perfectly in control. In the quenched red light he still saw the ruins of the painted imitation of a face which she wore and, underneath it, crumbling sandstone of her real appearance; under his fingertips, the coarseness of her skin and the melting ooze of her flesh spelled in braille she was a ruin of time. The tiny sharp whips of her dead bush of hair stung his face and eyes. But all this palpable evidence of decay inspired no revulsion, instead, a savage passion of tenderness; he wanted to reach the uncreated country of fountain and forest deep inside her, deep as the serene Beulah

114

Land where Viv once slept fleecily clad in lanugo down, under blue trees shedding fruit of light. She kept on screaming like a peacock, shapeless commands and beautiful strings of love words like necklaces of warm beads. So he reached near to Beulah and knew that so did she.

'Happy birthday,' his angel could not forebear to say at the river which is the boundary of that country; then, reaching at last for the other world, knew with marvellous pain it was gone or, all the time, a mirage, anyway. When she was silent and ceased to thresh about, Joseph heard the river sounds once more and discovered her bed smelled of face-powder and the hot-corn smell of spilled whisky. She was a prone statue, very white in the gloom because the covers were all this way and that way, some right off the bed. Seen so close, the texture of her upper arms was networked with satiny lines, like a veil clasped with the vaccination brooch.

'You can't ever take all your clothes off,' said Joseph, stroking her wedding veil. 'You'll always wear this.'

'It was quite nice, in the end,' said Mrs Boulder in a rain-washed voice, far away from him. 'It was worth waiting for.'

After another pause, she confided: 'You don't half get fed up with older men.'

'I dreamed I ate you,' said Joseph. 'You were in a glass dish and I attacked you with a spoon.'

'Did you really dream about me?' she said wistfully, sounding very young and sad.

'You swallowed me whole.'

But she had woken up. She swung her heavy thighs out of bed and rooted about for her negligee. Maternally she heaped up covers on Joseph. Then she looked down at him with a curious, half unhappy smile.

'All the same,' she said to herself, wrapping herself up, 'you are my Vivvy's friend and all.'

She clicked a switch beside the dressing-table and two frilly pink lamps on either side of the mirror shed a marshmallow light. She took cotton wool and cleansing cream from a huge array of jars, boxes and bottles and began to clean off her make-up.

'You'll have to see my poor face bare,' she said, scrubbing away, since she was no longer afraid to let him look at her. She stripped off the blurred colours. Joseph propped himself upright and watched her. He stole another cigarette from her bedside table. After their trip through space and time, he was interested now to find himself like a pretty boy in a French film smoking a faintly perfumed cigarette in a harlot's bed while its owner sat before a mirror working on her face. It was a very luxurious bed. The light was soft, diffuse and incredibly pink. He raised elegant hands as pink as roses and, laughing quietly to himself, formed a shadow kangaroo against the wall, which was papered in a regency stripe. She smiled at the kangaroo in the mirror.

'I always fancied you because you've got eversuch nice hands,' she said. 'I'm so glad the scars have almost healed. You can tell a lot by a man's hands. My Vivvy's hands, now, you can tell he's a musician.'

'Who was Viv's father? I've often wondered, Viv is so unnaturally happy. He must have a good hereditary.'

'I'll never know for certain,' she said collectedly. 'In fact, it's in rather bad taste of you to ask.'

'Come off it,' said Joseph. He made a shadow clergyman, who married them. They would live happily ever after. He felt ridiculously light of heart.

'Anyway, what does it matter?' she said. 'Father is only a word at the best of times but mother is a fact.'

'You mean, Father is only a hypothesis?' suggested Joseph.

'It was hard going at first but my boy, my Vivvy, made it all worth while.'

'You mean, Father is a kind of wishful thinking,' pursued Joseph. 'Screw you, Ransome, my father figure.'

'Mother knows best,' said Mrs Boulder obscurely. 'At first, oh, each time was a fresh violation. For years I felt degraded, I felt I was such a sinner I'd never be washed clean. But if death is the wages of sin, it's the wages of virtue too. And I was making such a lot of money, you'd never believe it. And no tax, either. And I thought, "Why am I a sinner? I am only doing a job of work and I'm not a liar, like priests, for example, who tell those lies." But my family was always Catholic and it's hard to lose a sense of guilt once it's been drummed into you. Once they've cast you for Magdalen, they'll never accept you as an honest businesswoman. So I took to the bottle, darling, the cowards' way out.'

She removed her false eyelashes with care. Joseph made a shadow of the knowledge of good and evil.

'Tell me about your family, if it won't upset you, I'd like to know about your family.'

'They were fairground people. Mum told fortunes, I learned to read off the Tarot pack instruction book but I can't tell fortunes myself, Joseph. I can't say what will happen to you. Honest, ducks, I hate to think, really.'

She examined her pale face now shining with grease and wiped it over with astringent lotion.

'I love you,' said Joseph, 'I adore you.' In the context or the room, the bed and the rosy darkness, it was true, as far as it went. She smiled vaguely.

'I'm very fond of both my boys. God, how trapped I felt when I knew Vivvy was on the way. I'd started out in show business, as a dancer. I had a nice figure, nice legs, I hadn't started to spread, then. Mum and dad had high hopes for me but first a fellow let me down and then one thing and another. It's no primrose path, you know. You wander about in a kind of daze, first one thing happens, then another, deaths and that. Then one fine day you wake up and you're an old woman living off your memories.

'I think of our mum and she'd tell our fortunes with the Tarot pack, me and my sister, who went to America and married a big Jew shopkeeper and Robbie my brother who got killed in the war, all us kids, and she'd tell our fortunes and I remember the cards, all greasy. And she'd say: "It's lies, don't forget." But when she drew a death for Robbie, she was everso upset because he was the eldest and the only boy. So now she's dead, and all. She used to call herself Madame Sophia and have a little booth with the signs of the Zodiac on it. Would you believe it, I'm Virgo. And mum would have a crystal ball but my dad worked the Ferris Wheel. Christ, I'm talking my head off. There's not usually anyone to talk to, you know.'

'Yes,' said Joseph.

'He worked the Ferris Wheel, the wheel of light. I'll tell you about my dad, he used to exhibit himself until he felt it was degrading, he had this tattoo on his back, it was a fox hunt with the fox disappearing down his hole. You get some marvellous art in tattooing. I knew an Irish labourer once with the Last Supper done in three colours all over his chest. But dad had a fall and hurt his back and our troubles began, our bad times started.'

'Listen,' said Joseph urgently, as if it were very important for her to know. 'I set free the badger. It was going mad in its cage and I set it free.'

She laid down a wad of cotton wool.

'What badger?'

'The badger in the cage. In the zoo. He went round like a needle stuck in a record groove, he was going crazy.'

'And you set it free?' she repeated, puzzled.

'I climbed over the wall and cut through its cage, yes.'

'Well, I never,' she said. She began to smooth on orange brown foundation cream. 'I thought it was Kay who set the badger free. Everybody said it was Kay.'

'Jesus, there's no justice,' said Joseph.

'Didn't you know that by now?'

'Don't do your face yet. It looks all withered with love.'

'With love. That's a joke. Do you love your mum and dad, Joseph?'

'I don't know,' he said, this time truthfully and with great pain.

'You ought to love your mother, at least,' she said.

He watched her daytime face growing again under her fingers, sad to see each stroke of her brushes take them further away from the glowing cave of room and bed. She was making her face impregnable once more.

'I have a date with a coloured gentleman tonight,' she said. 'Black as night but a lovely man. I haven't seen him for years, an old friend from the war-time, he was with the Free French. Oh, the chances I've missed, Joseph. If I'd played my cards right, I'd be in French West Africa, now, on the Ivory Coast in the lap of luxury.'

'Black is not as black as all that,' said Joseph drowsily.

'It's growing dark already,' she said, peeking between the curtains. Her face was almost finished. Her eyes were painted with the formal precision of those of the dead of Ancient Egypt. She picked up a brush to colour her mouth. She was almost an icon again.

'No regrets,' she said suddenly. 'No regrets, Joseph. It was good but you know it can't happen again so just go home and forget about it and I'll forget about it and –'

'You bitch,' said Joseph, stung. Outside, water splashed and a raucous chorus of seagulls wailed. 'Come here and I'll do you again, you bitch. After all, it's Christmas Eve.'

She put down the lipbrush and began to laugh. It was musical though not orchestral laughter; it was entirely childlike steam organ fairground urchin laughter. She shot across the room into his embrace like a plump human cannon ball.

Joseph crossed the road and began the climb home; at the mouth of the alley where, the previous night, he met Sunny, he came face to face with Viv.

'I've been looking for you everywhere,' said Viv. 'Where've you been? You look shagged out.'

'I've been screwing your mother,' said Joseph, at a loss for anything but the truth. He dodged past Viv, who stood open-mouthed, and began to run up the lane. After a few seconds, he heard furious footsteps behind him and, just outside Kay's house, Viv jumped on his back like the old man of the sea. Joseph crashed forward and for a moment or two they wrestled in the dirt, Viv punching at Joseph with all his might, but he was far too agitated to do harm, sobbing and cursing, and Joseph soon succeeded in catching Viv's wrists and restraining him.

'You bastard,' said Viv. 'You fucked my mother.'

He burst into tears. Joseph held him against him, curiously bored with the sight of yet more tears, overcome with the familiar sense of comic futility. He felt intolerably guilty to have made his friends appear ridiculous to each other.

'It was her birthday,' he said gently. 'And Christmas Day tomorrow, too. I'm sorry I was so thoughtless as to tell you.'

'I came to say they had announced a Christmas truce and all the time you were betraying me.'

'Betraying you?'

'Betraying my trust. I trusted you with her. I bet she was drunk and seduced you.'

'Perhaps,' said Joseph. 'It doesn't matter.'

'What do you mean, "it doesn't matter"! Do you mean you've

slept with my mother and it doesn't mean a thing to you?'

Joseph felt immensely tender to his friend; how would Hamlet have responded to discover Horatio in his shirt behind the arras in the bedroom scene instead of old Polonius? Above them, the fairy lights on Kay's balcony flickered on and off and there were carol singers, young children with sweet, thin, uncertain voices.

> 'The holly bears a berry
> As red as any blood.'

Viv wrenched himself free and got up. He looked more than ever like a sad monkey child.

'I wish you would go quite mad and be put away,' he said. 'That is my Christmas wish for you.'

He spat on Joseph, spat in his face and walked away; after a few steps, throwing his dignity to the winds, he broke into a headlong run.

7

J oseph went home, washed off Viv's saliva, made some tea
  and boiled some eggs, for he was very hungry. His cat was
at home and ate a whole tin of meat and gravy; then she sat
beside him in front of the fire, stuck one leg in the air and
washed her private parts. She was now as big as she could go.
Cautiously and tenderly, she licked her distended nipples which
had grown into long, blunt, pink nails of flesh. She had several
breasts ready to give milk and moved about clumsily. She
demanded attention with hoarse, imperious mews; Joseph
stroked her head and scratched behind her ears.

'Snow white,' he said, 'snow princess.' The cat purred ecstatically, writhing under his caresses; she did not know he would
act God with the fruit of her womb and disperse them. Because
there was a Christmas truce, no gunfire shattered the tranquil
meadow of December stars. And he still smelled sweetly of Mrs
Boulder, whose flesh had absorbed so many scents and perfumed lotions over the years it hardly seemed like flesh at all but
like an expensive laboratory product; she was a well-upholstered
science fiction craft who had hurled him into the interior of the
earth, where up is down, now he knew it for sure, an ultimate

disorientation, so black in her bedroom dogs would be scared to bark until they lit a fire. He was very tired and confused. He guessed that making love with Mrs Boulder had destroyed a pole of the world he never knew existed; now Viv struck him and spat on him, their friendship had irredeemably altered, perhaps to a more barbaric condition. He sat perplexed among his broken eggshells until Anne came tapping at the door.

'What's up with you?' she said, seeing his preoccupation.

'My brain is all over Paisley patterns,' said Joseph. 'I'm colourful but mixed up.'

'There you go again,' she said with distaste. 'Covering up your inadequacies with picturesque language.'

'You're an iron flower. I'll say that for you.'

She sniffed. She made no concessions to the festive season in her appearance, still armoured in grey flannel and chained with artificial pearl. She was stiff and stern as a moral precept, but she limped.

'I said I'd take you out, I recall,' said Joseph.

'That's right,' she said. 'You're not going back on your word, are you?'

Joseph was touched.

'Of course not. Only I am no longer friends with my friend so it will be an embarrassing party.'

'What, that bloke with the hat? What did you do to him?'

'I made a pass at his bird,' improvised Joseph.

'You can't think much of your friends, then.'

'So it would seem,' said Joseph. He buttoned up his threadbare overcoat, regretting Victorian shooting jackets, Eskimo anoraks lined with wolf fur and military greatcoats of the elegant past which Mrs Boulder remembered; all these now presumably decorating old men on the Down or bewildering the staff at Salvation Army hostels. Outside, it was a cold, brilliant night; the city lay curled up below like an animal infested with electric lights. All was calm, all was bright.

'The children will be getting very excited everywhere,' said Anne unexpectedly.

'I daresay they will,' said Joseph. 'It's quite an innocent time.'

'All that commercialization, though,' said Anne. 'That's hardly innocent, is it.'

'Do you want to have a white liberal conversation about the commercialization of Christmas?' demanded Joseph. 'If so, I'd far rather look at the stars, I tell you.'

'What do you mean?' she said, backstepping. 'What do you mean by "innocent"?'

Nobody had ever asked him to define the word for himself before. He looked at her stark, pale face.

'My cat kills birds innocently. How's that.'

'That's conventional,' she taunted. 'That's a cliché.'

'Some clichés only become clichés because they're true. Like "stone walls do not a prison make nor iron bars a cage". So now I'm starting to think perhaps Kay was right and we should not have let out the badger, that perhaps the badger was no longer fit for the outside world where people like you thought he would bite.'

'Don't try and get out of it, Joseph. Listen, would your cat still be innocent if she ate her babies like rabbits do?'

'Why not.'

'And what about me, what if I'd killed my baby because I couldn't stand it smiling at me?'

'Yes,' said Joseph slowly. 'You would be making your own terms, wouldn't you?'

'Then who's guilty?' she demanded spitefully.

'Lyndon Johnson,' howled Joseph like a wolf.

'Why is that? He can't help behaving like a politician, can he?'

'He hires men to do his murders for him and he never tells them it's murder. And some of them never find out. You know the story of the Emperor's new clothes; well, politicians wear executioner's hoods for so long as they turn into their faces and deceive everybody but children and madmen they are real.'

'You're not mad,' she said disdainfully.

'I know. I can tell a hawk from a bloody handsaw and what a disappointment it is. I'm sane and adult but I'm not going to fraternize, all the same.'

'I am a simple woman,' she said. 'You speak in riddles.'

He grappled with her tweed sleeves.

'Ask the assassins, they know hangmen only understand the language of the noose.'

'I knew you'd be against capital punishment,' she said, wrenching herself free. 'Even for those monsters who kill little children, hanging's too good for them.'

Joseph released her.

'Do you really think I should clamber back into society?' he asked, expecting no reply.

'After all, they've declared a truce in Vietnam, a truce for Christmas,' she offered tentatively, uncertain how he would react.

'The Buddhists must find it pretty inscrutable.'

'Why don't you get yourself a stand at Speaker's Corner?' she jeered.

His angel woke up again and demanded he try to violate her.

'Did you like sex, Anne?' he asked her in a diabolical voice. 'Tell me about your love life, did you like it when you got it?'

But he could not embarrass her nor crack her glaze.

'Not particularly,' she said in a perfectly neutral voice. 'I could take it or leave it and usually left it.'

The bushes and trees in the garden where the stone boy stood shifted and rustled as if softly applauding her abstinence.

'Is there nothing you care for, then?' he asked, remembering the ungainly dryad who clasped the buds of leaves.

'I had a window-box, in one of my rooms, once,' she said. 'I planted it with seeds. The birds came and ate them, I saw a sparrow, one morning, fly away with a seed in its mouth. I thought, what a cheek! And so nothing came up but I'd learned my lesson and never tried to grow anything again.'

'What seeds did you plant?'

'Nasturtiums. They're supposed to be easy.'

'You do conceal yourself heavily, don't you, you shrug around in this kind of camelhair dressing-gown all the time.' He had a vision of her gloomily cooking spare meals in unbecoming undress.

'I don't know what you mean,' she said with a note of fear. They were descending the hill; Joseph, a few steps higher than she, leaned forward heavily on her shoulders.

'If I had a real talent for immolation, I'd marry you,' he said.

'Oh, shut your cakehole, do,' she said, an insult from the primary school which refreshed and oddly comforted him. So they arrived at Kay's house, which blazed with lanterns and rang with music. A subdued roar of talk and laughter issued from the front door, which stood open; in the hall, the walls were covered with mirrors which distortedly reflected the party-goers in their gipsyish clothes of so many colours that, as they moved about, they seemed fragments in a giant kaleidoscope kept continually on the turn by a child's restless hand or pieces of disintegrated rainbow. A girl in white Levis and a hat with cherries and flowers on it cried out: 'Well, I never, it's Joseph Harker,' detached herself from the crowd and kissed him, although he could not remember ever having seen her before.

'I thought you were dead,' she said.

'I rose again,' explained Joseph. Anne looked at him askance.

The plan of the house was this: beneath their feet was a basement full of damp. On the ground floor were two stately tall rooms, one at the front and one at the back, overlooking a shrubby garden and the little lane, and the elegant hall where a languorously curved staircase rose up to the monumental first-floor drawing-room. This was a drawing-room out of Tzarist St Petersburg, suitable for informal dances, soirées musicales and formal receptions; there was a slightly smaller room at the front in the same grandiose style. The second- and third-floor rooms grew progressively smaller and less impressive and the house finally ended in a tangle of attics and lofts and cupboards and doorways that led nowhere. All this great pile of masonry and plasterwork belonged to Mrs Kyte, who had not left her bedroom for fifteen years; it was slowly and inexorably falling down.

Her son's friends carefully picked their way over floorboards friable with rot. Windows were either open for ever or closed for good for all the sashcords were broken. Cracked ceilings bowed and sagged. The single lavatory often refused to work. Rain came into all the attics. There was woodworm in all the wood. Wallpaper furled down most walls. The curvaceous staircase groaned, shook and trembled underfoot. The house was also curiously decorated and furnished.

Kay's mother lived in her theatrical past. She bought this dilapidated mansion for herself and turned it into a set for the major starring role never offered to her in the actual theatre. Its size and grandeur suited her pretensions and she never saw the decay. Under sedation in the upper room above the drawing-room, she relived triumphs she had never had; the house was full of enormous photographs of herself in silver frames with mirrors everywhere, now fly speckled and dusty, and huge, fringed velvet curtains stiff and blooming with dust and dirt and great urns and vases of Egyptian or Chinese design in niches, all bought up second hand.

In these antic surroundings of faked luxury and rampant neglect, Kay's floating world camped out. Mattresses and blankets sprawled on carpets worn down to the canvas backing. At night, each gilded papier mâché couch (with lion feet and faded red cushion) carried a freight of some dreaming young person. Toys, plants, comic books and stray articles of clothing littered rooms Kay and people continually passing through had painted with bursts of silver stars or grinning moons. Here and there throughout the house were these scraps of painting, flower forests, clouds and suns appearing strangely on walls papered with maroon flock or split pastel satins but nothing ever seemed carried to a conclusion, as though the artist or artists had got bored halfway through, idly dropped the brush and wandered off. Sometimes as much as an entire landing was covered in twining colours. Tonight, all the doors were open except that of Mrs Kyte's room. In most of the grates, fires burned. There was a smell of incense. They ascended to the drawing-room.

Four long windows opened on to the balcony where the fairy lights twinkled; beyond was a steep gulf of brilliant darkness, a view as from the prow of a ship. There were double doors to the other room; these had been thrown open so the main business of the party was taking place in what amounted to an enormous L-shaped baroque ballroom. In the short leg of the L, Viv and his friends were playing in a whirling blaze of flickering electricity. The marble fireplace, carved with a chastely sumptuous design of urns and garlands, roared with flames; swags and garlands of plasterwork topped the walls and all around the fireplace and the frieze were Woolworth's paper chains, pinned up as from the simple enjoyment of a riot of colours and shapes. More frills were twined round the artificial lemon trees which stood primly in pots between the long windows.

One long wall was entirely covered in pink tinted looking-glass from floor to ceiling, a fortunate buy from some luxurious dismantled ladies' powder room; the perspectives of the room, arbitrarily distorted by the mirror duplicated itself and seemed to chat and dance with its own reflection and this wall of mirror also reflected the windows and the trees and darkness outside, so the crowd appeared hemmed in on all sides by dangerous night. The reflected play of the lights of the band was like a show of silent fireworks. The heat and plangent music and the raised voices were so great the room throbbed.

Above the mantelpiece hung a very large oil painting of Mrs Kyte as a young girl, in a white dress, with a spaniel puppy, done in light colours and splashy brushwork of fashionable painters of the late 'twenties. On the mantelpiece itself, in a glass dome, was the very pair of dancing slippers worn by Mrs Kyte in her extreme youth on the single occasion she foxtrotted with the Prince of Wales. There was a photograph of the late Mr Kyte, the fighter pilot, who sported a handlebar moustache of dimensions quite beyond the capacity of his son. Also a great, shifting mass of used envelopes, letters, bills, postcards, gloves, shoes, coloured pencils, pots of paint, cigarette ends, cigarette papers, pieces of half-eaten chocolate, contraceptive packets and all manner of household detritus.

The heavy almond-green velvet curtains had been roughly streaked with gold and silver paints; the walls, originally coloured pink to tone with the mirror, were daubed with targets, fishes and tropical birds. To his pleasure, Joseph saw a picture of Prince Rudolph's blue bird of paradise. A light fitting consisting of a number of intersecting planes of opaque pink glass, relic of an abandoned super-cinema, hung in the centre of the room; this had been wreathed with plastic roses. Anne stiffly took off her coat and then her jacket and stood to attention with them folded over her arm. She seemed content to stand with her back against a piece of mirror and grimly appraise the company. She wore a beige cardigan over her white blouse. Joseph got her a beaker of draught cider; then he sat cross-legged on the floor beside her, gazing through a wood of legs.

'I've a sense of *déja vu*,' he complained. Though he had never been in Kay's house before, most of the faces around him swam in some distant sea of memory from before Charlotte left; the music, the draught cider slopping from the barrel on to the floor and jars of cheap red wine, these smiling faces everywhere stiff as the painted smiles of acrobats, all had once been over-familiar. Now it was strange to be among so many people, again, among so many people apparently enjoying themselves in fancy dress.

'Who do you think has come along as the Red Death?' he asked, but Anne did not hear him above the music.

Barbie, the American girl, was dancing in a backless silver lamé gown obviously borrowed from Mrs Kyte's historic hoard. Her marmalade mane, all stuck with artificial flowers, hung down her bare, sun-tanned tawny back and her lamé tail slithered like a fish; she was a wet mermaid. She was laughing and jingled with metal bracelets. Anne grunted derisively. It was about eleven, the time Santa sets out with his sleigh to descend chimneys; the Electric Opera finished their set and came from the L-shaped part of the room to get some drinks. Here was Viv.

'You rat,' he said viciously to Joseph. 'You swine.'

'Ladies present,' chided Joseph, dissociated through tiredness.

'Well,' said Viv. 'It's Orphan Annie.'

He began to smile; he wore his gangster suit and hat. The fat pearl in his tie glistened with the same lustre as his teeth.

'How nice to see you getting out and about and enjoying yourself,' he said to Anne in sophisticated tones.

Anne looked at him warily. There was a click and all the lights went out. The leaping firelight turned the tail of the American girl to burning gold and she was handing out sparklers to the revellers and they were all lighting them. Everywhere showered scintillating waterfalls of sparks, inside and outside the mirror. Viv took two sparklers from his jacket, lit them with an opulent new lighter and handed one to Anne; she watched it sputter into life. It was a magical thing.

'I haven't seen one of these for years!' she said. She made shimmering circles in the dark air; she laughed aloud. Her face took on a flimsy, borrowed radiance.

'You'll excuse me' said Joseph, glad to see her smiling. Anne and Viv were too busy lighting fresh sparklers to notice as he slipped away from the ballroom to find a warm place to sleep, as by now he could hardly think of going out in the cold for a cold walk to his miserable bed. On the landing, he met Mrs Boulder, accompanied by an enormous African at least six feet seven inches high and broad to suit, a glossy black in colour.

Mrs Boulder was wrapped in a white feather boa; her dress was tight white satin, split up one side, her spike-heeled shoes were silver and a silvery moon dust was puffed over her bouffant meringue of hair and her eyelids were silvered and her face was superb. She was entirely white on white, like a snowdrift in moonlight; she was a white queen and the African a black king. He wore a gorgeous robe of gold and crimson and a gold embroidered cap on his sculptural head. He had a wise and cynical face.

'Joseph, my darling!' she cried out, startled. Joseph saw the blue forest, the fountain, the tranced virgin and knew he would never go there again.

'I see your unicorn was black, as it turned out,' he said with extreme clarity; she thought he was drunk, she smiled.

'Pardon?' said the African with the trace of a French accent.

'Joseph,' she said gathering round her a magnificent regal composure, 'I want you to meet Toussaint, one of my oldest friends; my best friend, in fact, as it turns out after all these years.'

'Enchanté,' said the African, grasping Joseph's fingers firmly but gently with the hand that did not hold Mrs Boulder's arm. Even her fingertips were silver.

'Toussaint,' she said, 'this is my boy Vivian's friend, Joseph.'

'Behold, this dreamer, hein?' the African said, examining Joseph. He laughed hugely but with restraint, as if out of consideration for them sparing them the super-human blast of the entire laughter. Mrs Boulder leaned against his crimson shoulder and smiled. She was stone cold sober.

'Sorry, you've lost me,' said Joseph.

'It's a biblical allusion,' said Mrs Boulder sedately. She wore a new jewel, a diamond wristwatch. And had Joseph only dreamed of making love in this ivory tower and penetrating the mysteries of the woman in the moon, now, it would seem, appearing renewed next to a black, gold and crimson sun? Discomposed, he hastily excused himself again and darted off up the stairs while they made a stately progress into the ballroom.

He opened the first door he came to, stepped through and closed it softly behind him. He found himself in a dimly lighted room that smelled of sickness. Although the room reverberated with the renewed clamour of the musicians downstairs, it preserved a hushed calm. In a giant bed shaped like a scallop shell, above it and around it a drifting canopy of dirty gauze, a woman tossed and muttered. There was furniture made of glass everywhere and a big, old-fashioned radiogram. Kay was changing a record for his mother so she should have her own music; it was a hissy old seventy-eight. He lowered the pick-up.

'He dances overhead, on the ceiling near my bed ...'

The crystal diction of a female singer of the nineteen thirties, very sweet and cool.

'In my sight
Through the night ...'

Kay's shadow danced against the wall; he wore no special party clothes, only his horizon blue. The sick woman, his mother, stopped moaning to listen, washed up upon a reef of pillows; the noise of the Electric Opera beat gently against her like the Atlantic breakers of cheers and applause for triumphs she had never had.

'I whisper, "Go away, my lover, it's not fair",
But I'm so grateful to discover he's still there ...'

On her white satin bedcover lay a satin Pierrot doll, all soiled and torn. Kay poked up the fire for his sick mother. On the mantelpiece in a glass case was the little posy in a silver holder C. B. Cochrane presented to Mrs Kyte in her youth and beauty. The once pink roses and once white frill were now a uniform phantom grey. Joseph slipped out of the room as silently as he had entered it and climbed another flight of stairs, to the empty, lonely part of the house where the rooms were less pretentious, the ceilings low, the landings narrow. Joseph saw the plump girl, Rosie, walking away down a brown corridor. Mrs Kyte's random redecoration had not extended so far up her home and the only light was one mean bulb. Rosie was eating something and humming a tune to herself.

Remembering the Christmas truce, Joseph abandoned his desire to sleep and approached Rosie from behind. He put his left hand between her legs and ran his fingernail down the zip of her trousers. She gently pushed his hand away and turned round, continuing to eat whatever it was she was eating. She was wearing a man's singlet with a huge, cut-out heart appliquéd upon her left breast. She smiled at him dreamily. Her black curls tumbled around her rustic red cheeks. He slipped his right hand underneath the cut-out heart; her flesh was beautifully springy. She neatly rolled the paper of her Crunchie bar into a ball and threw it away. He replaced his left hand between her thighs; she moved up to him.

'Hullo, Joseph,' she said. She commenced to fumble with his clothes. 'It is Joseph, isn't it?'

'The world is so full of a number of things
I am sure we should all be as happy as kings,'

replied Joseph. They caressed each other. He pushed her against the brown wall. Her breath was sweet and thick with chocolate. She spoke once again, just as he was poised to enter her.

'Do something for me' she said.

'All right,' he promised, in no mood to argue.

'Say to me, "Rose, you are the most beautiful woman in the world".'

Joseph felt a jolt of such tenderness he thought his heart would break.

'Rose,' he repeated softly, 'you are the most beautiful woman in the world.'

She sighed with satisfaction, screwed her eyes up tight, don't look till I count three and I'll show you a secret, twining herself around him like a morning glory plant. When they drew apart, reeling and dizzy, he supported himself on the wall; the plasterwork gave slightly and a crack appeared. She smiled sweetly and dreamily at him.

'My mother is so fat she hasn't seen her feet for twenty years,' she said. 'I'm terribly afraid of growing fat.'

'I shouldn't let it worry you,' said Joseph, as reassuringly as he knew how.

'These things run in families, you know,' she said doubtfully. She adjusted her clothes, smiled again and wandered away, towards the staircase. She was tender and irreproachable as a cloud. In his dazed state, Joseph continued his search for a place to sleep.

Opening the nearest door, he found himself out on the roof, among the stars, on a small parapet with an overgrown pot of privet and a stone pineapple. There arose a great flapping of wings; dozens of pigeons who had been sleeping peacefully, heads sunk out of sight under feathers, perched around the chimneys and on ledges at the top of the house, were cruelly disturbed from their slumbers and soared and circled about. Then every bell in every church in the city began to peal out because it was midnight on Christmas Eve. The door banged shut behind him. He was suspended in crazy heavens between wings and bells.

Then, one by one, the birds plopped ponderously down on their perches again and began drowsily to coo as they rearranged themselves and the bells slowed down and stopped in the church towers and there was a luminous silence broken only by the sounds of the party far below. Joseph stayed on the parapet a little while longer, watching shadows of lights from the ballroom dancing against the trees in the garden and looking at the lighted windows in near and far terraces where just now mothers and fathers would be stuffing pillowcases with dolls, trains, jig-saw puzzles, nurses' outfits, toy pistols, chemistry sets, an apple, an orange and a handful of nuts. He thought of his dead grandfather. The remembered face was sepia, as in an old photograph; for the first time, he wondered if he had loved the old man because he was safely dead and could make no demands upon him.

He would have slept out on the parapet but it was far too cold. His fingers were numb and his face stiff; he retreated into the house. The light was off in the brown corridor. He groped along the wall until he found a door. Inside this attic, a candle burned on a plate. There was a mattress on the floor and a heap of army blankets. A handful of coals glowed in the grate. Vague shapes of tigers snarled on the walls. A discarded pool of silver and a mound of artificial flowers represented, he realized, the presence of the American girl, Barbie; she and Kay sprang up upon the mattress. Neither was wearing any clothes except for a string of coral and a latchkey on a string. Kay blinked without his shades.

'I'm sorry to disturb you,' apologized Joseph. 'I should have guessed the beds would be full tonight, no room, so to speak, at the inn.'

'Oh, we can always make room for you, Joseph,' said Kay courteously, pushing Barbie farther over the mattress. Joseph, all at once surrendering to the inexplicable, swung back and forth with the door and laughed. He laughed so much be became weak and limp. He laughed so much they caught the infection too although they did not know what the joke was. Kay curled into a ball and giggled hysterically and Barbie laughed like Doris Day, exhibiting perfect teeth; she clasped her slim, brown arms around her smooth, brown knees and laughed and her shoulders shook.

'Down the rabbit hole, again,' said Joseph; when he woke up, they were gone, the candle burnt away, the fire nearly out and the room in warm darkness. The blankets were carefully tucked round him and she had stuck her false daisies in his hair. Although he had not slept for more than a few hours, he felt quite renewed and ready for fresh surprises the night might bring. He folded the blankets neatly and went back into the corridor. A chorus of church bells tolled four.

There was no subdued party hum along the top landing, no sound at all, though the lights were still on. He went down the stairs; a huddle of young boys and girls sweetly slept on the threadbare carpet outside Mrs Kyte's door. He paused and listened; the gramophone was not playing but he could hear a woman's voice. He opened this door as softly as he had done before; the room was just as it had been, the glass furniture, the open fire, the satin doll, the featureless invalid in the rococo bed, but there was no Kay at the radiogram. Instead, Rosie, with her heart outside her bosom, sat by the bedside reading aloud in a flat, schoolgirl monotone, stumbling over the long words.

'No, I've made up my mind about it; if I'm Mabel, I shall stay down here. It'll be no use their putting their heads down and saying, "Come up again, dear!" I shall only look up and say "Who am I, then? Tell me that first and then, if I like being that person, I'll come up; if not, I'll stay down here till I'm somebody else."'

She was reading from *Alice in Wonderland*. Joseph found out that each night they took it in turns to read Mrs Kyte to sleep with stories from her childhood, *Little Women, What Katy Did, The Princess and the Goblin, At the Back of the North Wind, Alice, The Hunting of the Snark* and *Sylvie and Bruno*. She had to go so far back into her past to remember untroubled sleeps. A belated

French clock of gilt and brilliants gave out the hour of four with some melodious twangs, telling Mrs Kyte's slow time.

Sleepers crowded the stairs like the pigeons on the roof and there were spilled drink, broken glass, dropped food and cigarette butts everywhere. On a plywood archbishop's chair, covered with turquoise brocade, Joseph discovered the Irish girl Maggie, Prince Rudolph's original blue bird of paradise, who had somehow made the party and now slept deeply, with her melodeon on the carpet beneath her. The house buzzed with dreams. The ballroom was still warm and fragrant but only a few survivors sat quietly among the wreckage of the party and the heaps of dreamers, who reappeared in the extra dimension of pink mirror like those slain and prone on the battlefield the morning after the battle.

The Black King and the White Queen were gone. The Electric Opera slept among their fallen instruments except for Viv, who was at that moment pouring tea into thick white mugs from a big brown pot for Barbie, Kay, Anne Blossom and old Sunny. Joseph was surprised to see Anne had stayed the course. Her hair was a confusion of wire wool and there was an irregular shaped stain on the front of her cardigan. She was cutting bread and butter; all kinds of things to eat were arranged on a tea tray. If Joseph was surprised to see Anne, he was quite astonished to see Sunny, who wore his outdoor coat and cap in defiance of the fire and held a fiddle in one hand while, in the other, he held a thick ham sandwich. First he took a large bite from the sandwich; then he laid it down and took a mouthful of tea. He greeted Joseph with a nod.

'I live down the basement,' he said. 'Always have. Lived there forty years. You never knew that, did you.'

'I never did,' said Joseph. Perhaps he was only imagining the fiddle. He did not dare touch it, in case it was not real.

'Lived down the basement for forty years,' Sunny repeated in a fatly self-contented voice. 'She bought me with the house, see. Rent act. Tee hee, tee hee hee. Rent act. You never knew I lived along with Kay.'

Joseph accepted tea.

'You saw her Black Prince, did you,' said Viv. 'I got home in such a state, I was so upset, and there he was, large as life, larger; they were sitting there like love birds and she looked like a young girl, blushing, and now she's going off to the Ivory Coast with him and leaving me and says she's cutting the apron strings, at last, it was time I was on my own. I tell you, my lover, I was everso cut up. And I'd wasted all my emotion on you and couldn't respond properly.'

He was blurry with resignation. He had taken off his tie and unbuttoned his shirt, revealing much black hair.

'So I expect I'll learn to forgive you, in time, least said, soonest mended, even though I learn that, not content with my mother, you slipped that Rosie a crafty length. You're certainly making up for lost time, aren't you. But then, it's the season of goodwill.'

'Give us some more char,' said Sunny; Viv filled his mug.

Joseph wondered what had happened to Anne Blossom, if she had had love or visions. Her face was pale but stern. Barbie no longer wore the silver dress but a loose smock of brilliant printed fabric, her feet were bare. She watched pictures in the fire; there were peacock feathers in her hair, now. Joseph sat beside her.

'Who's your angel, Barbie?' he asked. 'What's your scene?'

'Flesh is grass,' she said absently, as if repeating the lesson for the day.

Joseph felt it might be doomsday tomorrow. He thought thankfully that perhaps he was forgetting how to think or feel except with his senses only. He examined the labyrinthine pattern of his ten whorled fingertips, possible maps of a new world.

'What's the enemy?' he asked her, sure she would reply.

'Time,' she said immediately. 'He's here, there and everywhere and he always wins out in the end.' She pronounced the vowel in 'time' in a round, appetizing, American way.

'Put me among your souvenirs,' he said, fingering her coral necklace. She laughed her high-school cheerleader laugh and looked so healthy, normal and full of gaiety and colour Joseph was enchanted. She unwound her peacock feathers, took a comb unexpectedly from the bosom of her dress and combed out her hair.

'Didn't you try to make explosives or something?' she asked. 'I heard some kind of strange story. Kay said you were dead but you wouldn't lie down.'

'I'm going to throw away my book of facts,' he said. Then old Sunny, having finished his sandwich and swallowed the last of his tea, stood up. He flourished his violin, which really existed.

'Rosin!' he demanded. Kay, who had been toasting a slice of bread, dropped the fork and rummaged in the mess on the mantelpiece until he found the amber cube of rosin. Sunny rosined his bow and flourished it.

'I'll christen it with a tune,' he said. 'My lovely new fiddle, my best Christmas present ever, thanks to Kay. Ta, Kay, ta, son. My lovely present.'

He commenced to tune up. A soundly sleeping boy in Red Indian costume was sufficiently disturbed to roll away into a corner. Kay began to butter his pile of toast. He looked like Loblie-by-the-fire, a household sprite. His shades were pushed up on his forehead. They ate toast, jam and ham sandwiches.

'I played before crowned heads such as "The Rose and Crown",' announced Sunny, standing straight up with the fiddle under his chin. 'Now, from the ridiculous to the sublime; "Air on the G String", by Johann Sebastian Bach.'

And he really could play the fiddle. Grunting, sweating and heaving, he nevertheless proceeded to play the air on the G string with much vibrato. The sweet, rich melody strung out upon the air like motes of honey or drops of gold and Sunny's fingers quivered on the strings. He dwelled with love upon each swelling note and arrived slowly, sweetly at the conclusion with such a depth of feeling they were all silent in the silence that followed and Sunny peered anxiously around, upset to be robbed of the praise and applause that were his due. But Rosie, who had slipped into the room unnoticed as he played, rushed up to him, kissed his withered cheeks and embraced him.

'I never heard such music, grandad,' she said. 'That's what I call a tune. Not like this modern rubbish.'

Sunny was radiant with delight and beamed like the sign of the Sun Insurance Company, perhaps how he had first gained his name. He had more tea and more sandwiches, clutching hold of his fiddle all the time.

'I bet you played really great when you were young, just like you said,' Anne told him. She was stiffly apologizing for her previous rudeness. 'I bet you played like a real maestro.'

'I did,' said Sunny contentedly, extending his boots towards the fire.

'I always thought you lived mainly in your old coat,' said Joseph.

'You were wrong, weren't you,' said Sunny, sucking and mumbling contentedly on a crust.

Kay piled more fuel on the fire.

'This night is cold as charity,' he said.

'You don't say much,' said Joseph to Kay.

'What do you expect me to say?' replied Kay. 'I haven't got a talking mouth.'

He had a small, thin, gently smiling mouth. It was, indeed, a quiet mouth. His face, close to, was quite old and very much creased and wrinkled. Now Joseph could find it in his heart to forgive him for being happy.

'You should smile more,' he said unexpectedly to Joseph. 'Personally, I make a point of smiling at least once every half hour, even if nothing pleasant happens.'

'I'd have to persevere,' said Joseph doubtfully. 'You need to be tough as hell to follow a regime like that.'

Viv and Rosie were asleep. Their faces were soft and defenceless. Barbie's eyes were closing; her comb tangled in her hair.

'The world is full of horrible and inscrutable inhumanities,' said Joseph. 'Can you keep on smiling every thirty minutes surrounded by these snakes and lightenings?'

'Do you see him?' asked Kay, indicating the photograph of his father, the war hero. 'Mr Kyte the fighter pilot. He also took part in the fire raids over Dresden. I read all the books about them, for years I was obsessed with it and thought I lit those flames myself; he was my father and I keep him, now, where I can keep an eye on him. But the dead stay dead, down in the black.'

Sunny yawned and laid down his fiddle.

'Did you say black? You see old ma Boulder's beau, black as your hat, blacker? What's she doing with a black man, eh? Eh?'

'Fornicating,' explained Kay benignly. 'I should think, at this time of night.'

'Big black bugger!' complained Sunny. 'What a size! Of course, women go for niggers on account of their choppers, it's well known, what a size!'

He yawned again. Extreme age had returned his face to the spontaneous transparency of childhood; he was sleepy and happy for all to see. He hugged his fiddle to his breast.

'Goodnight, ladies and gentlemen,' he said. 'Goodnight, goodnight.'

For a finale, he played 'I'll see you in my dreams', then sank down like all the others, still embracing his violin even in sleep.

'It was nice of you to give him a fiddle,' said Joseph.

'*You* never thought of that,' said Kay, faintly accusing. 'Now they are all fast asleep except for you and me and Anne, poor Anne with her poorly leg.'

She raised her head. She and Kay exchanged a long stare. The wind sucked and moaned. Coals shifted on the fire and the paperchains rustled.

'Poor Anne,' repeated Kay in an odd, strained voice, as if he had caught sight of something extraordinary, the possibility of something utterly outside his experience. He stood up hesitantly and took Anne's hand. The little diamond sputtered with light. Some silent chord struck in the vast room; a ripple of strangeness seemed to stir the hair on the heads of the sleepers. Joseph found he was breathing hard and digging his nails into his palm. He crouched hunched up watching fey, delicate Kay pull clumsy Anne to her unwilling feet. It was the time of the winter solstice, one of the numinous hinges of the year.

'Anne,' said Kay, almost in a whisper, a hoarse, secret, lover's whisper, 'walk straight. I think you can walk straight, tonight, if you try.'

'What's that?' she said. 'What?'

'Wake up, Anne, and walk down the room. Walk!'

'I can walk but I shall limp,' she said.

The wind whistled and sparks flew up the chimney. The visionary green eyes of Barbie's peacock feathers flashed out and the only people awake upon the round world were Joseph, Kay and Anne in a magic ship of light upon an ocean of darkness. Horizons diminished round them. They were alone.

'You won't limp if I say you won't,' said Kay, blazing with conviction; he held her tightly, his small body appeared to throb in an ecstasy of vehemence. She had to lower her head a little to be on a level with him; her face showed weariness and doubt and at last a willingness to be persuaded, like a rush of love.

'All right, Kay,' she said in a thin, young voice. 'Don't shout at me.'

He expelled his breath with a hiss.

'Walk down the room with me and don't limp,' he said. 'You're not going to limp for one step.'

He took hold of her arm and they set off, while Joseph knelt in the cinders, watching them absorbedly, as if his life depended on her walking one foot before the other, one, two. Very slowly, she walked with such stiff legs he could not tell if she were limping or not.

Now they appeared in the mirror, a strange couple repeated twice, two wizened boys, two coarse-boned girls. Slowly, slowly all four continued down the room. And now Joseph saw she was not limping at all but, as they progressed and she gained more confidence, was even walking with a certain grace, even walking tall and hardly leaning on Kay any more.

'Walk by yourself,' commanded Kay, releasing her arm. 'Walk by yourself, now. You can.'

Terror flashed briefly across her features; she swayed dangerously but did not fall and gradually drew herself up to a handsome height and completed the walk to the end of the room with the proud steps of a racehorse coming into the field.

'Run!' said Kay. 'Run back to me!'

She turned and ran towards him. She was laughing exultantly. Then she ran right back to the fireplace and spun round and back to Kay, racing her mirror image.

'I'm all right again,' she said. 'It wasn't a punishment for what I did.'

'Did you think that, Anne?' asked Joseph, shocked he had not guessed.

'Oh, yes,' she said, 'I thought they made me lame to punish me for giving myself away. I thought they'd punished me for that.'

She continued to run backwards and forwards for several minutes. Her heavy shoes made a subdued clatter on the worn pile of the dark red velvet carpet. Backwards and forwards. Kay came slowly back to Joseph. He produced a half empty bottle of red wine from behind a chair and drank some. His hands were trembling so wine spilled on his jacket. The he passed the bottle to Joseph and began to roll himself a cigarette but dropped all the tobacco out of it and had to start again, made another mess and then pettishly threw all the makings down.

'She had hysterical paralysis,' he said. 'Anybody could have cured her, anybody who said to her in a firm enough voice, "Nonsense, you don't really limp at all." Not a miracle. No miracle. It wasn't a miracle. Was it?'

Anne continued to run up and down, now rippling with laughter like a quiet brook.

'My father,' said Kay, 'who aren't in heaven. I hate your lousy face and always have.'

He seized the photograph from the mantelpiece and pitched it bodily into the fire; the glass broke in two.

'And I didn't really care about her at all!' he said to himself, as though he could not comprehend it. 'I just had an intuition my voice would reach her, that's all.'

Outside, the old woman began to shake her mattress; the first white feathers of snow floated down more softly than dew and churches began to chime for five o'clock. Anne came to a standstill at last, in front of the dying fire; she pulled off her little ring and threw it among the embers.

'Finders keepers,' she said.

'I should burn the lock of hair,' suggested Joseph, for whom the room was incandescent.

'I'd planned to,' she said. She was flushed from her exertions. 'While I was practising running, I was thinking: "I'll burn that lock of hair, it's morbid to keep it." Oh, what a Christmas morning!'

'I'm friends with time again,' said Joseph, not realizing he spoke aloud.

'Everybody wins and we all get the prizes,' said Kay. He sounded desiccated, worn out. He picked up the bottle of wine. He said with beautiful politeness: 'Forgive me leaving you for a while; I shall go and sit with my mother.'

He wavered as he walked as if he were a piece of trick photography and might suddenly disappear altogether, so discreetly the air would not even be disturbed by his passage. As if his goodnight act were to cast sleep upon them, both Joseph and Anne lay down and closed their eyes as soon as he was out of the room, both, in their different ways, perfectly content; already this marvellous happening seemed quite natural, like the existence of Sunny's violin, incorporated into the actuality of the house. Everyone in the room slept but, once again, Joseph did not sleep long. He dreamed the fire went out and he was cold and, when he woke up, he was cold because the fire was out. It was a simple dream and came true.

The room was now full of snow light, shining back with a double brilliance from the great mirror. Whiteness was everywhere; three or four hours of snowfall laid the city out in the whitest of sheets and all the distant hills were sumptuous white beds or colour contour elevations and plans of Mrs Boulder's body. Seagulls hooped and hovered over the deserted river. Nobody moved in the ballroom yet. Viv and Rosie lay in each other's arms, like Daphnis and Chloe. Orange russet locks of Barbie's hair crept like ivy over Anne's arms and throat for the accident of sleep brought them close as lovers. Nobody moved in the whole house as Joseph crept through on his way out into the frosty morning, where most of the other world was already awake. There were smells of bacon and glimpses of festive parlours with tinselled trees, and children, snugged up in wool, were coming out to make snowmen or try out new tricycles.

Joseph climbed the stairs to his own room; his cat was sleeping in his blankets and purred a symphony to see him home, thrusting her head deep into his bosom as he stroked her swag belly, the little breasts and silky underparts. He judged she would be a mother again in a few hours. He thought he had never seen anything so beautiful as her almond-shaped green eyes. He carried her out with him on to the parapet, cleared a place in the snow and sat at the top of the morning, holding the purring cat on his knee. He looked over the bowl of morning full of snow. There was some terracotta sunlight. A few children played in the garden below, beneath the stone boy whose eyes were blocked with snow and who wore a snow helmet on his head. Joseph put the cat into his room and pulled the windows shut to keep her there; he stood up and stepped on to the low wall of the parapet, half eager to let his body follow his mind into free fall. He saw his shadow blue upon the snow-covered pavement and raised his arms above his head like a diver about to launch himself into eternity. He was put out to see Dr Ransome's kind, tired face appear out of the sky and knew him angrily for a hallucination.

'Don't come bothering me,' said Joseph. 'You are only an emanation, a soothe-me. A soothe-sayer. Go away and look after the sick people.'

Dr Ransome's kind smile never faltered but his face immediately began to fade away. Then Joseph clambered back over his windowsill, gave his cat food and milk, lay down on his bed and fell into a profound sleep. When he woke again it was the violet dawn of another morning and a tremendous purring was going on at the foot of the bed; his cat sat smiling and purring like an aeroplane about to take off giving suck to five kittens all as white as snow and beautiful as stars.

March–December 1967

VIRAGO MODERN CLASSICS
&
CLASSIC NON-FICTION

The first Virago Modern Classic, *Frost in May* by Antonia White, was published in 1978. It launched a list dedicated to the celebration of women writers and to the rediscovery and reprinting of their works. Its aim was, and is, to demonstrate the existence of a female tradition in fiction, and to broaden the sometimes narrow definition of a 'classic' which has often led to the neglect of interesting novels and short stories. Published with new introductions by some of today's best writers, the books are chosen for many reasons: they may be great works of fiction; they may be wonderful period pieces; they may reveal particular aspects of women's lives; they may be classics of comedy or storytelling.

The companion series, Virago Classic Non-Fiction, includes diaries, letters, literary criticism, and biographies – often by and about authors published in the Virago Modern Classics.

'A continuingly magnificent imprint' – *Joanna Trollope*

'The Virago Modern Classics have reshaped literary history and enriched the reading of us all. No library is complete without them' – *Margaret Drabble*

'The writers are formidable, the production handsome. The whole enterprise is thoroughly grand' – *Louise Erdrich*

'The Virago Modern Classics are one of the best things in Britain today' – *Alison Lurie*

'Good news for everyone writing and reading today' – *Hilary Mantel*

'Masterful works' – *Vogue*

VIRAGO MODERN CLASSICS
&
CLASSIC NON-FICTION

Some of the authors included in these two series –

Lisa Alther, Elizabeth von Arnim, Dorothy Baker, Pat Barker,
Nina Bawden, Nicola Beauman, Isabel Bolton, Kay Boyle,
Vera Brittain, Leonora Carrington, Angela Carter, Willa Cather,
Colette, Ivy Compton-Burnett, Barbara Comyns, E.M. Delafield,
Maureen Duffy, Elaine Dundy, Nell Dunn, Emily Eden, George Eliot,
Miles Franklin, Mrs Gaskell, Charlotte Perkins Gilman,
Victoria Glendinning, Elizabeth Forsythe Hailey, Radclyffe Hall,
Shirley Hazzard, Dorothy Hewett, Mary Hocking, Alice Hoffman,
Winifred Holtby, Janette Turner Hospital, Zora Neale Hurston,
Elizabeth Jenkins, F. Tennyson Jesse, Molly Keane,
Margaret Laurence, Maura Laverty, Rosamond Lehmann,
Rose Macaulay, Shena Mackay, Olivia Manning, Paule Marshall,
F.M. Mayor, Anaïs Nin, Mary Norton, Kate O'Brien, Olivia,
Grace Paley, Mollie Panter-Downes, Dawn Powell,
Dorothy Richardson, E. Arnot Robertson, Jacqueline Rose,
Vita Sackville-West, Elaine Showalter, May Sinclair,
Agnes Smedley, Dodie Smith, Stevie Smith, Christina Stead,
Carolyn Steedman, Gertrude Stein, Jan Struther, Han Suyin,
Elizabeth Taylor, Sylvia Townsend Warner, Mary Webb,
Eudora Welty, Mae West, Rebecca West, Edith Wharton,
Antonia White, Christa Wolf, Virginia Woolf, E.H. Young

'Found on all the best bookshelves' – *Penny Vincenzi*

'Their huge success is solid proof of the fact that literary fashion is
a snare and a delusion – people like a good old-fashioned read' –
Good Housekeeping

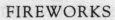

FIREWORKS

Angela Carter

'Fizzing with allegory, symbolism and surprises' – *The Times*

Here is the ritualism of Tokyo where lovers ponder intangible reflections of themselves, 'reflections of nothing but appearances, in a city dedicated to seeming', and 'the velvet nights spiked with menace' of a wasted London, poised on the brink of destruction. In these extraordinary tales Angela Carter pinpoints the symbolism of city streets and weaves allegories around forests and jungles of strange and erotic landscapes of the imagination.

THE PASSION OF NEW EVE

Angela Carter

'If you can imagine Baudelaire, Blake and Kafka getting together to describe America, you are well on the way to Carter's visionary and lurid world' – *The Times*

New York has become the City of Dreadful Night where dissolute Leilah performs a dance of chaos for Evelyn. But this young Englishman's fate lies in the arid desert where a many-breasted fertility goddess will wield her scalpel to transform him into the new Eve. *The Passion of New Eve* is an extraordinary journey into the apocalyptic vision of one of Britain's most brilliant writers.